Flash

Soulless Kings MC
Book 9

Andi Rhodes

Blue Journey Publishing

Copyright © 2023 by Andi Rhodes

All rights reserved.

No part of this book may be reproduced in any form or by any electronic or mechanical means, including information storage and retrieval systems, without written permission from the author, except for the use of brief quotations in a book review.

Cover Artwork - © Amanda Walker PA & Design Services

Edited by Darcie Fisher.

For Amy...
Thank you for hopping on the crazy train and becoming an integral part of my team!

Also by Andi Rhodes

Broken Rebel Brotherhood

Broken Souls

Broken Innocence

Broken Boundaries

Broken Rebel Brotherhood: Complete Series Box set

Broken Rebel Brotherhood: Next Generation

Broken Hearts

Broken Wings

Broken Mind

Bastards and Badges

Stark Revenge

Slade's Fall

Jett's Guard

Soulless Kings MC

Fender

Joker

Piston

Greaser

Riker

Trainwreck

Squirrel

Gibson

Flash

Royal

Satan's Legacy MC

Snow's Angel

Toga's Demons

Magic's Torment

Duck's Salvation

Dip's Flame

Devil's Handmaidens MC

Harlow's Gamble

Peppermint's Twist

Mama's Rules

Valhalla Rising MC

Viking

Mayhem Makers

Forever Savage

Saints Purgatory MC

Unholy Soul

A note from the author

First, thank you from the bottom of my heart for loving Soulless Kings MC so much that you've made it to book #9! When this series began, I had no idea it would become a world I would get lost in for this long. It's been a roller coaster for sure, and as it nears the end, I'm filled with so much emotion. Goodbyes are never easy, and this one will be especially hard. I guess it's a good thing there's one more story to tell after Flash. Royal would not sit quietly by and be forgotten.

That being said, are endings in a book ever really endings? Something to ponder...

Second, one thing you might have realized throughout my books is that I always take on difficult topics. I don't sugarcoat things, no matter how hard they might be. And I am not a fan of trigger warnings, as I never want to spoil any part of a story, even the most taboo of things. But even I have my limits and my own set of triggers.

When I dove into the lives of Flash and Jaci, I had a story I wanted to tell. Unfortunately, it's not my story. It's theirs. And let me tell you, they had a slightly different and vastly more emotional version they demanded to be told. I fought it at first, wanting to protect myself from their trauma, but it was impossible. So I will do what I can to protect you, my readers, without giving too much away.

Flash is an addict. That's no secret, and not a spoiler, as it's in the blurb. His journey through addiction is just that: his journey. As the family member of an addict, it was hard for me not to intermingle my own story into his, but I prevailed.

And then there's Jaci. Be warned, she is fierce and so damn strong, but she's flawed like every human on the planet. Her story, their shared story, is emotional, gut-wrenching, and yes, triggering.

If you want specific information on triggers, please do not hesitate to reach out to me via email or social media. I am more than happy to go into detail privately. What I will say is this: if abortion is something you can't read about, even in fiction, then this isn't the book for you. And rest assured, that's okay. No book is ever for every reader.

Please note, Flash is a work of fiction. It is not a commentary on the social and political climate, or my own personal beliefs. It is not meant to offend or upset anyone. It's just a story… Flash and Jaci's story.

So, now that I've 'warned' you, go grab a box of tissues, a bottle of wine (or whiskey if that's your preference), and enjoy!

Much love,
Andi

Prologue

I just need to forget.

Flash
Sixteen years old...

"I don't want to go."

I raise myself up on my elbow and stare into her eyes. It's still early for a Saturday night, but Jaci's parents are strict, and she has a curfew more suited for a twelve-year-old. If Jaci were anyone else, I'd beg her to stay, to forget the trouble that awaits her if she's late. But she's not someone else, and I refuse to be the reason she spirals into one of her depressive episodes. I love her too much for that.

"I know." I thread my fingers through hers. "I don't want you to go either. But you have to."

Jaci yanks her hand from mine and jumps up from my bed to pace. I know she's mad, but what's the point? Her parents are never going to change. We need to bide our time until we both turn eighteen and then we can get the hell away from this town, from them.

When Jaci stops pacing, she faces me and there's no mistaking the tears that are welling up in her eyes. I scramble from the mattress and wrap my arms around her.

"Hey now, don't cry," I soothe as I rub circles over her back. "You'll see me tomorrow, I promise. I'll be waiting on your porch for you to get home from church like I do every Sunday."

Jaci quietly sobs into my shirt. She mumbles incoherently, and I let her, not bothering to try and make out her words.

"I hate them," she says when her crying subsides. "Why can't they just let me be normal?"

"Because parents suck. But they're only trying to protect you."

"From what?" she cries. "You?"

I shrug. "Probably. We don't exactly come from the same side of the tracks."

"Just because you didn't grow up with money doesn't mean you're bad news." Jaci has never looked down on me, has always defended me against anyone who dares to treat me like I'm less than because I don't wear the nicest clothes or have the newest things.

I reach for Jaci's hand and tug her toward me to tuck her under my chin. "You are the only one who thinks so. And I love you for it."

She tips her head back and rises to her tiptoes. "I love you too," she says before kissing me.

At sixteen, I have little to no restraint. I groan as the tip of her tongue darts between my lips, seeking entry. Deepening the kiss, I pull her along as I back up toward the bed.

Flash

We both topple onto the mattress when the back of my knees hit it, but we don't stop our teenage lip lock.

When I slide a hand under the hem of her shirt, Jaci arches her spine to push her boob into my palm. I rub my thumb over her nipple, teasing it into a hard peak. I swallow Jaci's moans, and with each one, my dick jerks in a plea to be inside her.

"Wyatt!" Jaci and I are startled apart by my father's shout. "Boy, get your ass down here!"

His words are slurred, telling me he spent the last several hours at the bar. He's probably lining up cocaine chasers on the coffee table again. That seems to be his routine lately, ever since Mom left us high and dry two years ago. How he's still alive, I have no idea, but I'm glad he is... although I'll never admit that out loud.

I rest my forehead against hers. "Two years, babe. Then we'll be free." I don't know if I'm reminding her or myself at this point.

Jaci nods, and when my father yells for me again, she rolls her eyes. "You better get down there."

"Wyatt!"

"I'm comin' old man," I yell back.

I grab Jaci's bag off the bed and slide it over her shoulder. Then I grab her hand and we head downstairs. Just as I suspected, my father is sitting on the edge of the ratty couch, and he's bent over snorting what appears to be his second line through a straw.

He inhales deeply before shaking his head. Neither Jaci nor I say anything, trying to get to the porch without him spotting us. I can feel the nerves coursing through her, and I squeeze her hand to remind her I'm here with her.

"Oh, would you look at that?"

With my hand on the doorknob, I twist to glare at the man whose DNA makes up half of mine.

Maybe I'm not so glad he's alive.

"Jaci, sweetheart, why don't you come over here and let me show you what it's like to be with a real man?" His eyes linger on my girlfriend's tits as he licks his lips lecherously.

My vision blurs at his words, and anger takes over my thoughts. I let go of Jaci's hand and slowly move around her to face my father.

"Apologize to her," I seethe, my hands clenched into fists at my side.

He laughs. "Now why would I do a stupid thing like that? She's just like any other slut, willing to spread her—"

Adrenaline fuels my actions and masks the pain when my fist connects with his mouth. His head snaps back, blood spurting from his split lip. He tries to straighten, but I hit him again. And again and again.

"Wyatt, please stop."

Jaci's voice, calm and beautiful, breaks through my rage. My hand is frozen in midair. I look at my father and see that I've beaten him unconscious. I return to Jaci's side and lift her hand again, not even thinking about the blood that's coating my knuckles.

"He's not worth it," she says quietly.

"No, he's not." I turn and tip her chin up so she's looking into my eyes. "But you are."

Jaci's eyes slide closed for a second, and she takes a deep breath. When her eyes open, there's no mistaking the sadness in their golden depths.

"C'mon. You need to get home," I remind her, even though I know that won't chase away the sadness.

Jaci hugs me like she always does, but there's something off about her hold. She pulls away and averts her eyes.

"You'll be there after church tomorrow?"

"I always am."

Jaci lifts her gaze to mine. "Good. I, uh..." She clears her throat. "There's something I want to talk to you about."

"You're not breaking up with me, are you?" I tease, but there's nothing teasing about the panic clawing its way up my throat.

"What?" She shakes her head. "No, I'm not breaking up with you."

I exhale the breath I didn't realize I'd been holding. "Good. Because you're it for me,

Jaci. Always."

"And you're it for me. Forever."

I shift so I'm facing the street where her car is parked at the curb. "You should get going.

I don't want your parents to have any reason to be upset with you."

She pecks me on the cheek and dashes down the steps. When she reaches the driver's side of her vehicle, she calls out, "Love you."

"Love you too."

I wait until her vehicle turns off my street before going inside and locking the door. My father is still passed out, so I return to my bedroom. After locking the door, I strip out of my clothes and add them to the pile in the corner.

I don't know how long it takes me to fall asleep, but when I do, it's filled with dreams about what Jaci wants to talk to me about. Even my subconscious is nervous. Every horrible scenario haunts my sleep.

The next morning, I wake up late. Stumbling to the bathroom, I quickly shower and dress. I find the living room empty. Apparently, my father wasn't too wasted or hurt to get himself to bed, which is a step in the right direction.

Usually, I have to guide him down the hall and shove him face first into his mattress.

Grateful for one less task, I clean up the white powder he left on the coffee table and add it to the baggie that still remains on the couch. I used to toss whatever he left out, but that resulted in him attacking me with a broken beer bottle and several stitches in my scalp. I don't throw shit away anymore.

After setting the baggie on the small dining table, I heat up a few pop tarts and grab a Dr. Pepper out of the fridge. I text Jaci to let her know I'm running late, but the message bounces back as undelivered. Thinking there's a service issue, I pocket my cell and head out.

I eat my breakfast and listen to music on my cell phone while I walk to Jaci's house. I have a rusty Chevy S-10, but it needs new brakes, and I don't have the money to do that.

Two hours later, I'm walking up Jaci's driveway. The garage doors are shut, so I can't tell if the family is home yet, but I see that there are no lights on inside, so I assume they aren't.

Maybe they stopped at the country club for brunch.

I walk up the steps to sit on the porch but freeze in my tracks when the front door comes into view.

"What the hell?" I mutter to myself.

The door is open a crack, which is so out of character for the Stines. Normally, the house is locked up like Fort Knox, even when they're home. I race inside, not even pausing to consider the danger that could await me. My only priority is to get to Jaci and make sure she's okay.

Nothing looks out of place in the entryway, other than the key hook by the door is empty. I quickly traipse through the first level of the obnoxiously big house, calling Jaci's name every few seconds. I don't get a response, and no one shows their face.

By the time I reach Jaci's room, my heart is hammering out of my chest. I try to call her phone, but all I get is a cold, robotic voice telling me that the number is no longer in service.

"Jaci! Where are you, babe?"

Silence is the only response. Motherfucking silence. Terror rides shotgun as I move into her attached bathroom, searching for anything that will tell me what's going on. Again, nothing. I make quick work of checking the rest of the bedrooms before backtracking to the first floor.

The security room is off the kitchen. Mr. and Mrs. Stine had cameras installed in every room, as well as outside, after a break-in last year. I've never given it much thought, but I am now. So much fucking thought.

I try the knob and, finding it locked, ram my shoulder into the door. The hinges give out so I'm able to kick my way in. The monitors are on and cover one wall in the room. My eyes flit from one to the next until I land on the image of Jaci's room. The camera is placed so you can see into the bathroom, at least as far as the counter. The toilet and shower are out of view.

I find the coordinating controls for that monitor and rewind it until I see Jaci on the screen. I note the time and see that it was before the family would have left for church. She's frantically throwing clothes into suitcases, swiping her cheeks every few minutes, and her father is standing a few feet away, an angry scowl on his face as he watches her. My blood boils at my girl crying. I rewind it further to try and figure out what happened and why she's packing. She said nothing about a trip her family was taking.

About fifteen minutes earlier, Jaci is standing in the bathroom doorway staring at what appears to be a slip of paper. She's startled by something or someone and whips her head toward the door to her room. Within seconds, her mom is there, yanking the paper out of Jaci's hand.

Jaci tries to get it back, but she can't. Mrs. Stine slaps her across the face and a shouting match ensues. Four minutes later, Mr. Stine walks in. His wife shoves the paper into his chest, and he holds it out to read it. After crumbling it into a ball and tossing it into the trash can, he returns to Jaci.

When I see the shouting continue, I can't help but wish there was sound. I watch the rest of the tape until Jaci and her father leave the room, each carrying two suitcases. Needing to know what was on that piece of paper, I run upstairs and grab it out of the trash.

I smooth the paper and my eyes lock onto one word: pregnant.

Son of a bitch!

Jaci's gone. They took her away from her home, her friends... me. I try to talk myself out of believing that I'll never see her again, but I fail miserably. There is no way in hell her parents found out she was pregnant, with my baby no less, and simply took her on a vacation to celebrate.

No. They're punishing her. And by punishing her, they're punishing me.

I leave the house with a lead ball settled in my gut. Images of Jaci flash through my mind, memory after memory assaulting my senses. I hold onto those memories, those visions of good times we've had, because deep down, I know they're all I'll ever have.

The walk home goes by in a blur, and by the time I

reach my house, all I want to do is forget. That's the only way I'll survive the kind of pain losing Jaci inflicts on my heart.

I spot the baggie of coke on the table, right where I left it. I hear my father's snores from down the hall. Everything here is normal, exactly the same as it was just over four hours ago. But I'm not. Nothing about how I feel is normal. My life will never be the same again.

I just need to forget.

I stare at the baggie as if it holds the answers to surviving life without Jaci. Because I don't know that I'll survive, at least not if I remember. I meant what I said to her last night. Jaci was it for me, always.

Without giving it too much thought, I snag the baggie off the table and take it to my bedroom. I lock the door and move to dump the contents onto my dresser.

I just need to forget.

Tears well in my eyes as I imagine Jaci standing next to me, hearing her voice telling me not to do this. Once I have the coke lined up, I hesitate. Jaci's voice remains clear in my mind, begging, *pleading* for me to stop, to think about the consequences.

I just need to forget.

I push her words aside and focus on my own subconscious.

I just need to forget. Make me fucking forget.

With tears slipping down my cheeks, I lean forward and snort the white powder. It takes more than a few minutes for the effects to kick in, but when they do, I realize I made a huge mistake...

Cocaine might make me feel good for a short time, but it doesn't help me forget. Instead, it increases the panic.

And the panic sinks its talons into every fiber of my being and demands more.

So. Much. More.

Chapter One

I am an addict. And I will always be an addict.

Jaci
Present day...

"You almost done for the day?"

I swivel in my chair to look at Tina, my best friend and business partner. We opened You Got This Recovery a little over a year ago and our lives haven't been the same since.

"I've got one more intake at five-thirty," I tell her, knowing it's not what she wants to hear. "Why?"

"Seriously?" she pouts. "Why would you schedule an after-hours intake on your birthday?"

I lift the file I started from my desk. "This is why."

Tina sits down in the chair across from my desk and picks up the file. I watch her face as she reads the details of our newest patient. It isn't hard to tell when she reaches the one detail that I'm never able to overlook.

"Well shit," she mutters. Tina locks eyes with me, and

her expression softens. "I'll stick around until you're ready to go."

I shake my head. Tina and I met in the boarding school my parents enrolled me in after they ripped me from the only home I'd ever known, away from the person who meant the world to me. She knows all the nitty-gritty details of that time in my life, and she's never once judged me.

Maybe that's why You Got This Recovery works so well. Between her family history of addiction and my struggles with pain medication in my late teens, focusing our lives on helping addicts was a no-brainer.

"Go home, Tina. I'm fine." I smile, but it's as fake as the diamond ring I wear to ward off obnoxious assholes at the bar when we go out... and Jaci knows it. "I'll call you when I'm done, I promise."

Tina snorts. "Yeah, no. Thirty is a big deal, J. There's no way I'm taking the chance that you'll go home and wallow like you do most birthdays."

Rolling my eyes, I concede. "Fine. Wait here if you insist. Then we'll go out."

The bell dings in the lobby, alerting us that our new patient has arrived. I hear Megan, our receptionist, greet the new arrivals. Bickering ensues as Summer, the girl I know I'm going to have to watch my boundaries with, gets berated by her parents for *being incredibly irresponsible*. Their words, not mine.

"Sounds like they're a barrel of laughs," Tina comments as she stands up. "I'll be in my office catching up on charting. Get me when you're done."

I agree to do that, and Tina leaves. I grab Summer's file and head out to the lobby. I force a bright smile and ignore Megan's 'brace yourself' look.

"Mr. and Mrs. Kish, I'm Jaci," I say, holding my hand

out for them to shake. Then I turn toward my new client. "You must be Summer."

The teenager averts her eyes, staring at the floor like it holds the secret to getting out of here. She shuffles her feet, and the tension in the room thickens.

"Summer, the lady is talking to you," Mrs. Kish bites out.

The lady can handle this, thank you very much.

"It's okay, Summer," I say gently. "I know this can all be a little overwhelming."

"It's not okay," Mr. Kish snaps. "She had no problem communicating in order to get knocked up or to talk to a dealer, so she can—"

"Summer, why don't you come with me?" I position myself so it's clear that my focus is Summer and only Summer. "We'll talk for a bit and then, as long as you're comfortable, I'll invite your parents back to chat."

Summer's eyes dart back and forth between her parents and me. Her lips are parted in surprise, but she nods.

"Good." I turn to Mr. and Mrs. Kish. "If you'll have a seat, we won't be too long."

I wrap an arm around Summer's shoulders and guide her to my office, ignoring a blustering Mr. Kish. I'm guessing it's not often he's essentially dismissed. Fortunately, I've had practice with fathers like him.

After closing my office door, I urge Summer to have a seat on the small sofa along the wall, which she does. When I sit across from her, I notice she's fidgeting with her hands.

"How long has it been?" I ask.

Her head snaps up. "Huh?"

I smile and clarify. "Since you last used? How long has it been?" She looks away. "It's okay, Summer. You can be honest with me. There's no judgment here." Still, she doesn't respond, and I sigh. "Six years, eight months, and twenty-two days. Before that, it was five years, seven months, and four days."

Summer finally faces me with a shocked expression. "You were an addict?" she asks softly.

"I *am* an addict," I correct. There was a time I couldn't admit that without feeling paralyzing amounts of shame, but I've grown a lot since then. "And I will always be an addict. But I'm no longer in active addiction."

"Oh."

"So, how long has it been?"

Summer swallows, and I swear I hear the thunk of her throat. "Um, like, almost a day."

"Okay, good. That means you haven't used anything today." I make a note in the file. "I was told that your drug of choice is heroin. Is that true?"

"Um..." Summer nods.

"Can you tell me a little bit about how your addiction started?"

For the next hour, I try to coax information out of Summer, but she's closed off. It's understandable, and she reminds me of myself so much that I know when not to push. After I finish with her, I invite her parents to join us. Mrs. Kish does, but Mr. Kish refuses and waits in the car.

By the time I've finished the intake, given the tour of our facility, and gotten Summer settled in, it's almost eight-thirty. I'm exhausted but I promised Tina I'd go out with her, and I won't back out.

"Damn, that was a long one," Tina remarks when I walk into her office. She narrows her eyes as if assessing how much damage this particular client is going to cause me. "You okay?"

I rub my temples. "Yeah, I'm good."

Flash

"Liar."

She rises from her chair and walks around her desk toward me, grabbing her purse off the rack on her wall as she passes it.

"Really, Ti, I'm fine," I insist.

"I call bullshit," she says brightly. "But I'm gonna let it slide since it's your birthday. Problems can wait until tomorrow." She links her arm through mine. "Celebrating cannot."

Thirty minutes later we're walking arm and arm into our favorite bar. Tina is cheerful, which is typically the case, but I can't stop thinking about Summer and...

Don't go there, J.

Chapter Two

Booze would've been the safer bet today.

Flash

"Where's the rest of the money?"

I glance down the alley for the third time, but my anxiety doesn't lessen even after assuring myself I wasn't followed. It's been a while since I've bought from a stranger, and the slight shake of my hands reminds me of that fact every second I'm standing here.

"What the fuck do you mean, the rest?" I snarl. "You told me fifty bucks."

The piece of shit shifts his eyes to take in my Harley. "That was before you rode up on that." He smirks. "The price has since doubled."

This would be so much easier if I were wearing my cut. No one fucks with a Soulless King. But I'm not here as a brother, and if word got out that a Soulless King was buying cocaine off the street, our credibility would tank.

"Fine." I pull another fifty out of my wallet and slap it against his chest. "Now gimme the powder."

He reaches into his pocket and pulls out a baggie. Gripping it between two fingers, he holds it in front of my face. "Pleasure doing business with ya."

I snatch it from him, barely containing the urge to snort the coke straight from the plastic. Today, of all days, my ability to be patient is as shocking as a nun in a whore house would be.

It's just another day.

Only it's not. This date will never be *just another day*. Because today is Jaci's birthday. Her thirtieth to be exact. And no amount of booze, pills, or cocaine is going to make me forget. Trust me, I've tried.

You're still trying.

I tip the baggie and spill some of the powder onto the back of my hand, almost dumping the entire thing on the ground when my cell phone vibrates in my pocket. Carefully, I pull out my phone and see Fender's name flash on the screen.

"Yo," I say by way of greeting.

"Where are you?" he snaps.

"I took a ride down the coast."

It's not a total lie. And it's what I do every year to avoid being around my brothers when I spiral. I'm what the experts call a functioning addict, but there are certain dates that are impossible for me to functionally survive.

"Well, get your ass back to the clubhouse," he barks. "We've got a run, or have you forgotten?"

Shit.

I did forget, but I will never admit that. "I remember. Heading back now."

Fender hangs up, and I groan as I slip my cell back into

my pocket. So much for doing my best to shut out the world. I glance at my hand and shrug.

One little bump won't hurt.

An hour and a half later, I'm riding alongside my brothers, itching for another hit. It doesn't help that the product we're running is in *my* saddle bags... taunting me, tempting me, calling out to me louder than the remainder of the eight ball in my pocket ever could.

But my demon will have to wait. My brothers haven't figured out my secret, and I don't intend to let it out of the bag today.

We arrive at the meeting location, and Drake, our buyer, is already there. He's standing outside with Looper, one of his goons, and they're both standing there like sentries as we park next to the building.

Fender, Joker, Riker, and Royal start toward the door.

"Meet us inside," Fender orders me before stepping through the doorway and signaling Drake and Looper to follow.

I quickly gather the product from my saddlebags and tuck the drug-filled duffel under my arm. My demon claws beneath my skin, begging to be fed. Any other day, and I could ignore it, but not today.

Scanning the parking lot, I reassure myself that I'm alone, and then reach into my pocket for my baggie. I set the duffel for our buyer on the ground at my feet before tapping some powder onto my hand and snorting it.

As I bend to pick up the duffel, the door to the warehouse opens, and Royal pops his head out.

"You comin'?"

"Yep."

I stride in his direction, ignoring the assessing look he

Flash

gives me, but before I can slide past him, he grips my arm. I glare at his hand and then level my gaze on him.

"Might wanna wipe that shit off your nose before you go inside," he says casually.

My eyes widen. "Oh, uh, thanks." I rub my nose on the sleeve of my shirt.

"Don't mention it."

Royal releases me and stalks down the hall to the room where we normally meet up with buyers at this location. I follow, doing my best to put one foot in front of the other as panic swirls in my gut.

Did Royal see me?

Will he say anything to Fender or any of the other brothers?

How do I force him to keep his mouth shut?

Question after question tumbles through my mind, none of which I like the answers to that my coke-hazed brain comes up with.

"Took ya long enough," Fender comments when I enter the room.

"I had to piss," I snap.

"Fucker gave whole new meaning to the road name Flash," Royal grumbles. "Saw way more of him than I ever cared to see." He looks at Joker. "Next time you're going to get him."

Okay, so he has my back so far.

"Jesus, lay off the coffee," Riker adds. "I swear you drink more of that shit than anyone else in the world. Makes you piss too much, and you're jittery as hell sometimes."

"Boys," Drake interjects. "I'm a very busy man, so I'd appreciate it if we could get down to business."

"Sure thing," Fender says. He nods at me. "Give him the product."

I toss the duffel to Drake, which he catches easily.

"This feels light," he says as he tests the weight of the bag.

Out of the corner of my eye, I see Royal tense.

"It's all there," I assure him.

Drake snaps his fingers and Looper steps up beside him. He slams the duffel bag into Looper's chest. "This seem light to you?"

Looper hefts the bag into his arms. "Sure does, boss." He tilts his head. "Not by much... but enough."

"Like Flash said, it's all there," Fender says, his tone low and menacing.

Joker and Riker flank Fender, and all three of them have their hands on their weapons. Drake and Looper exchange a look, but neither of them draw their guns.

Drake grins, but there is zero humor in it. "This has been a great partnership, Fender. You supply the product, we sell it, and we both make money."

"Your point?" my president asks.

"My *point*," Drake begins. "Is that I associate with people I trust. I've always trusted the Soulless Kings." He shrugs. "But now? I don't know."

"Nothing has changed in the way we handle our business," Joker snarls. "That duffel isn't light. It's the same amount you've purchased from us for the last five years."

"Maybe," Drake concedes. "Maybe not. The fact remains that until I weigh it, I won't know. And I don't like walking out on a deal when I don't know exactly what I'm getting."

"Look, *Drake*." I sneer his name, unable to stay quiet any longer. "If you're having second thoughts, then say so. But don't you dare question the integrity of our club. That won't end well for you."

Flash

Drake lifts his hands in mock surrender. "No disrespect intended, gentlemen." He lifts his chin at his goon. "Give 'em the money."

Looper reaches into his jacket pocket and pulls out a thick envelope. He hands it to Riker but holds onto it a little longer than necessary. Drake and Fender stare each other down.

"If I find out you've screwed me, there will be consequences," Drake says.

"Understandable," Fender concedes. "But we haven't screwed you." Fender lifts his hand in the air and makes a circle to indicate we're done and leaving. "I'll be in touch."

With that parting remark, the five of us walk away. Once outside, we stand by our Harleys. It's only when Drake and Looper come outside and then leave the lot that we relax.

"What the fuck was that?" Joker asks, glaring at all of us.

"Drake knows his shit," Riker says. "If he says that duffel was light, it probably was."

"My thoughts exactly," Fender says flatly. "Club meeting in two hours. Attendance is mandatory."

* * *

As I stare at my reflection, I take deep breaths to ward off nausea. I know I have nothing to worry about as far as the product Drake was given today because that wasn't me. But the way it all played out has me realizing how lucky I've been up to this point.

I reach into my pocket for the last of my coke but find the baggie open and empty.

Son of a bitch!

Digging my fingers into the lining of my jeans pocket, I try to scrape some residual powder from what spilled. There isn't nearly enough to make snorting worth it, but I do it anyway. Then I splash some cold water on my face and head out to the bar in the main room to wait.

"Hey, handsome," Margo greets me when I slide onto a stool. "What can I get ya?"

"Nothing."

"Aw, c'mon," she prods. "I know there's a meeting soon and all, but a little shot of somethin' won't hurt ya."

If she only knew.

"I'm good, Margo." I force a smile. "Thanks though."

"Well, if you change your mind, let me know."

As I sit and wait for everyone to arrive for the meeting, I stare at the rows of liquor bottles behind the bar. Booze would've been the safer bet today. And bonus, I could've drunk enough to pass out versus snorting my fucking thoughts away and needing one fix after another to keep myself comfortably numb. Not that I ever reach numb.

"Flash!"

I turn my head to look over my shoulder at the sound of my name. Fender is standing at the end of the hallway that leads to his office and the room where we hold church. Piston is standing just behind him, a scowl on his face.

"Office, now," Fender orders before turning and walking away.

Piston stays rooted in his spot. The panic that's been hovering all day sinks its teeth in and bile rises up the back of my throat. I swallow it down and slowly make my way toward Piston.

"What's going on?" I ask our VP.

Piston doesn't respond, but rather whirls around and strides into Fender's office. I follow, but when I step over the threshold, the bile I tried so hard to keep down shoots up my throat. I turn just in time to puke in the hallway, rather than on the office floor.

When there's nothing left in my stomach to purge, I face the two highest-ranking Soulless Kings. Both Fender and Piston are leaning back against Prez's desk, arms crossed in front of them. Prez stares at me like he has no clue who I am, while Piston's scowl remains firmly in place.

And sitting on the couch along the wall, with an apologetic tilt to his lips, is Royal.

"So, Flash," Fender begins. "Anything we should know?"

Chapter Three

That person has occupied way too many of my thoughts over the last fourteen years, and I refuse to give him my hungover ones as well.

Jaci

Cotton balls.

Yep, that's what I'm tasting. Dry, fluffy, disgusting cotton balls.

Groaning, I try to sit up, but my head spins and all the alcohol I consumed last night at the bar threatens to make an appearance. I try to lick my lips, but it's pointless. There is absolutely nothing wet still in my body. The booze made sure of that.

A piercing wail splits the air, and for a brief moment, my brain screams fire. But then I realize it's my alarm. Why I have it set for the weekend is beyond me at this particular time, but I'm sure I'll remember once I'm feeling more human.

I roll over and immediately regret it when I fall to the floor with an oomph.

"Son of a bitch," I mumble.

How much did I drink last night?

"A lot," I answer myself. "You drank like a damn fish because you couldn't stop thinking about—"

No! No, no, no.

That person has occupied way too many of my thoughts over the last fourteen years, and I refuse to give him my hungover ones as well. If only it were that easy.

I manage to get up on all fours without upchucking my stomach, and I crawl to the attached bathroom. Apparently getting drunk at thirty is completely different than getting drunk in your twenties because I don't remember *ever* being so out of it that I had to crawl.

The small window in the bathroom provides enough light for me to see, but barely. I use the vanity to pull myself to my feet, swaying slightly when I'm upright. Once I'm steady enough, I brush my teeth, savoring the minty fresh toothpaste.

After I pee, wash my hands, and pile my hair into a messy bun at the top of my head, I return to the bedroom to put on something more than panties. Dressed in leggings and my favorite hoodie,—the one thing from my past my parents didn't take away—I make my way into the kitchen for coffee.

While the pot is brewing, I lean under the faucet to wash down some Tylenol. I debate on breakfast, but the mere thought of food sends ripples of nausea through my stomach. After filling my mug, I retrace my steps to my bedroom to grab my cell and then head into the living room to sit on the couch with my legs tucked under me.

I open my texts and am struck with the reminder that, aside from You Got This staff, Tina is the only person who wished me a happy birthday. Not even my parents took the time out of their judgmentally busy lives to do so. I shouldn't be hurt by their slight because I told them years ago that I wanted nothing to do with them, but I can't help how I feel.

As always, thoughts of my parents ignite the bitter fury that simmers just beneath my skin at the immense amounts of pain they've caused me. The past overtakes the present until I'm lost in a memory.

"Jaci, we're going to be late for church."

My mother's voice barely penetrates through the giddy haze fogging my brain. I initially read the words on the piece of paper I'm holding and was shocked. But that was three days ago, and I've had time to adjust.

"I'm coming," I call out to her.

When I realized my period was a week late, I'd peed on a stick. And when the result was positive, I went to the local clinic to confirm.

Pregnant.

I read the word over and over and over again. At first, the word shocked me. Wyatt and I always use a condom, and I'm on birth control. I guess our health teacher was right about the only thing one hundred percent effective is not having sex at all. But that's not nearly as fun.

I've hopped, skipped, and jumped from one emotion to the next, coming to terms with what is happening. Having a baby as a teenager is not what I imagined for myself, but with Wyatt, I know I can handle anything.

I wonder what our baby will look like. Will they have my eyes or Wyatt's nose or my hair? Lost in thought, I startle when my bedroom door opens and whip my head around to see my mother coming toward me.

"What in heaven's name is taking you so long?" she

Flash

gripes. She snatches the piece of paper from my hand and scans the words. When she looks at me again, her face is pale. "What is this?" she asks as she shakes the paper in my face.

I try to grab it back, but she yanks her arm back to hold it just out of my reach. "It's nothing."

"Nothing?" she practically screeches. "This says you're pregnant. Is it some kind of joke?"

I lower my head, knowing that no matter what I say, my mother is going to be pissed and mean.

"Answer me when I ask you a question," she snaps.

"It's not a joke, Mother."

"This can't be happening. You're sixteen. You're a virgin!"

I can't stop the smirk tilting my lips at her blatant disregard for what is staring her in the face. "Obviously not."

Stinging pain travels through my cheek when her palm connects with it. "Don't you dare get smart with me, young lady."

I don't react to the slap, or to her screaming for my father. I knew I wouldn't be able to hide this from them forever, but I was hoping to tell Wyatt first and then, I don't know... run away with him.

"What is going on in here?" my father demands when he enters my room. "Why are you shouting?"

Mother hands him the confirmation slip I got at the clinic. Father's face reddens, and his shoulders stiffen.

"What is the meaning of this?" he asks as he shakes the paper in my face.

A shouting match ensues, accusations are flung around like debris in a tornado, and life as I know it is irrevocably changed.

The ping of a text notification pulls me out of my head.

I swipe at the tears that always flow when I'm lost in the past so I can read the message.

> **Tina: Have you ever heard of the Soulless Kings?**
>
> **Me: Who hasn't? You can't exactly live in Oregon and not know who they are.**
>
> **Tina: Have you ever met any of them?**
>
> **Me: I've seen them riding around on their motorcycles. But I've never actually met them. Why?**
>
> **Tina: It seems one of them is coming to YGT. Coke addiction. And get this...**
>
> **Me: What?**
>
> **Tina: They're paying in cash. Paid extra for a private room, too.**
>
> **Me: Seriously? Who the hell is this guy?**
>
> **Tina: His name is Flash... well, that's what they call him. They refused to give me a legal name.**
>
> **Me: Sounds sketchy. Are you sure we should take him on?**

Tina: It's already done. I accepted him into the program this morning. The guy I spoke with... the president I think... he said Flash had to go to rehab or he would lose his patch. Girl, I've seen Sons of Anarchy. I was not going to be responsible for whatever shit they did to him if it came to that.

Tina and her stupid shows. I've never watched Sons of Anarchy, but she's told me all about it, and I wouldn't want to be responsible for that shit either.

Me: Okay. I'll get him in on Monday for an initial individual session. Do you need me to head in to do the intake?

Tina: It's my on-call weekend. I've got it. You get some rest. If you're feeling half as hungover as I am, you need it.

Me: Oh yeah... I'm never drinking again. EVER!

Tina: We'll see. Love ya.

Me: Right back at ya.

I close out my texts and open the scheduling app we use at YGT. After adding Flash into my already busy Monday afternoon, I decide to watch some TV. Tina and I alternate on-call weekends, and I always try to make the most of my time off. And by make the most of my time I mean be as lazy as humanly possible.

Scrolling through the shows I can stream, I come across Sons of Anarchy. I suppose now is as good a time as any to see what I'm going to be up against with my new client.

Chapter Four

Get up! Get up and face your demons.

Flash

Two nights.

I've been at You Got This Recovery for two fucking nights, and it sucks donkey balls. When Fender gave me the choice between rehab and losing my patch, the decision was a no-brainer. I'd be lost without the Soulless Kings. But this isn't exactly a bucket-list vacation.

"Mr. Flash?"

I roll my head toward the door and glare at the man standing there. "It's just Flash, Sam," I tell him for what feels like the hundredth time. He's the only staff member I've met, other than Tina, the co-owner of YGT. "Quit adding the 'Mr.'"

"Right." Sam walks into my room, a private one thanks to the club's deep pockets, and stands at the foot of the bed to stare at me. "The therapist has you on her schedule for one this afternoon. Once you meet with her, you'll have a treatment plan, which will allow us to determine which groups you'll benefit from, as well as any other activities that might be good for you."

"Okay."

"Look, I know rehab is hard. Especially the first few days, or even weeks, but it will get easier. Once your mind is a little clearer, you'll see."

"My mind is already clear," I snap, annoyed that he's treating me like every other junkie that comes into this place. "My drug use doesn't affect my ability to function."

"Yet here you are."

"I'm here because I have to be." I throw my legs over the side of the bed and sit up, twisting my neck so I can still see him. "I'll do the work because I have people in my life who need me to, but I'm not like the rest of the people you treat."

Sam walks to the door, but before he exits, he looks over his shoulder. "Maybe you're more like *those people* than you think."

With that parting comment, he disappears into the hallway. I glance at the clock on the wall and groan when I see that I've got four hours until I meet with this therapist chick. Four hours to do what?

A whole lotta fucking nothin'.

When I arrived on Saturday, I signed a few papers, met with Tina and Sam, and was given a tour before being dumped in my room. I haven't left the confines of these four walls since, and I'm going insane. I've eaten meals in here, have an attached bath, and I'm not able to attend groups until I meet with the therapist. All that leaves me with is a ton of time stuck in my head, thinking about things that only cause cravings.

Flash

It's a vicious cycle.

Needing to kill time and keep myself busy, I snag my cell phone from the generic nightstand. Tina tried to take the device away from me, but Fender managed to convince her to allow me to keep it. It goes without saying, she was less than thrilled.

I scroll through social media for a bit, and once I'm bored with that, I switch to text. I read the message Fender sent yesterday to check up on me. He kept it short and sweet, and I didn't respond. I didn't know what to say. But I can't ignore the man forever, so I tap out a quick reply.

Me: Doing fine. Wanna get through this so I can get back to the club.

Almost immediately, three dots start bouncing on the screen. My mouth quirks up on one side at how quickly he's replying. Fender isn't one of those presidents who lords over his men. He genuinely gives a shit about all of us. We're family. I imagine he's had a death grip on his phone since he hit send yesterday waiting on me to text back.

Fender: Don't ever keep me waiting that long again... I'm glad you're ok. Do you need anything?

Me: Heard, Prez. Unless you can snap your fingers and rewrite history, I'm good.

Fender: You got this.

I roll my eyes at his obvious attempt to keep things light-hearted when he is typically anything but.

Me: Right. I'll check in later.

Fender: Don't worry about things here. Do what you gotta do to get home.

Me: I will.

Fender: I know.

To say I was shocked when I wasn't immediately booted from the Soulless Kings is an understatement. In the years since I've become one of them, it never dawned on me that another option would be given. Granted, I had no intention of anyone ever finding out about my addiction, but now that the cat's out of the bag, a weight I didn't even realize I was carrying has been lifted off my shoulders.

Too bad another weight can't be lifted.

My addiction is one thing... the reason I started using in the first place is another. Rehab can't fix that. Fuck, nothing can. I'm forever damned to lug that particular baggage around.

In an effort to keep my mind occupied, I turn on the television and flip through the channels. Back at the clubhouse, we have a satellite, and the viewing options are endless. Palms may have been greased here, but it doesn't change the shitty cable TV. I make a mental note to ask Fender to bring my streaming stick when he visits.

If he visits.

Just because I was given the option to come to rehab

doesn't mean that any of my brothers will give me the time of day while I'm here. Sure, Fender is texting, but that doesn't require much effort or time. Visiting does.

I settle on the news but barely pay attention as my mind wanders like it always does when I'm bored. So lost down the black hole of my memories, I don't even hear the knock on my door or Sam entering my room. I'm unaware of him until he snaps his fingers only inches from my face.

I smack his hand away. "What?" I bark.

"It's time for your session with the therapist."

I glance at my phone to confirm, not that I think he'd lie to me. It's habit for a man like me. I work with money and numbers, both of which require accuracy. Double-checking things is second nature and not something I'm likely to ever stop doing.

"Let's get this over with," I huff as I stand.

Sam leads me through the building, and I pay attention to all the details I missed when I first arrived. The rehab facility is decorated homier than most, not that I've ever seen the inside of one before. I can see what appear to be cabins through the windows, each one different from the last.

"Here we are," Sam says when he stops outside a door. "You can have a seat and she'll be out to get you in a minute." He points to one of three chairs lining the wall to the left of the office.

"I thought you said she was ready?"

"No, I said it was time for your session," he informs me.

"Same thing," I mutter under my breath as I sit.

Sam crosses his arms over his chest and stares down at me. "You've got a chip on your shoulder the size of Texas. I suggest you work on that."

"I was working on it."

"Using drugs isn't what I meant."

"No shit," I snap. "I'm an addict, not a goddamn idiot. But I think I'll reserve my talking for the therapist if it's all the same to you."

Sam chuckles, but there's no humor in it. "If you think she's going to be easier on you, think again. Ms. St—"

Sam presses his lips into a firm line when the office door opens.

"I'll take it from here, Sam. Thank you."

That voice... I'd recognize it anywhere. It's got a sultry edge to it that wasn't there before, but it's the same voice that's haunted my dreams and every waking moment of my life for the past fourteen years.

No.

"No problem, Ms. Stine," Sam says with a smile before walking away.

"Now, Mr. Flash, if you'll come inside, we can get started."

The therapist disappears inside her office, leaving me sitting there like a dumbstruck jackass. My brain screams at my legs to lift me up and carry me inside, but I remain frozen.

Get up! Get up and face your demons. Or the cause of your demons anyway.

"Mr. Flash?"

Fuck. I close my eyes and take a deep breath. I push away all the pain and heartbreak that's currently threatening to swallow me whole.

Rising to my feet, I square my shoulders and step inside the office. I halt just beyond the doorway, not quite capable of making my way to the chair across the desk from where she's standing.

Flash

She hasn't lifted her head to look at me, and I'm guessing she didn't really pay attention in the hall, or this interaction would be vastly different. Taking another deep breath, I mentally brace myself for how my words are going to be received.

"You can just call me Flash... Jaci."

Chapter Five

You got this.

Jaci

"You can just call me Flash... Jaci."

I shake my head slightly as I keep my focus on the file on my desk. I must be losing it because I'd swear the voice of the man in my office belongs to Wyatt King. But that's not possible. Fate can't be that cruel.

Fate is the cruelest bitch there is, and you've experienced that firsthand.

"Get it together," I mumble.

"Shouldn't you be telling me that?"

I lift my head, fully prepared to be proven wrong about who the voice belongs to, and my heart slams into my ribs at Mach speed. My head spins, and I sway, only managing to stay upright by gripping the edge of the desk.

"W-Wyatt?"

Flash

His face hardens to what should be an impossible degree.

"Wyatt died a long time ago," he says as he takes a step forward, then another. "It's Flash now."

"Flash?"

He shrugs. "I didn't pick it."

He didn't pick it? What's that supposed to mean? I open and close my mouth several times, but no words come out. Wyatt—no, Flash—tips his head as if to study me. He must not like what he sees because he scowls.

"Nope. I can't do this," he snarls. "I agreed to rehab for my addiction, not a total reckoning for my entire life."

Flash whirls toward the door, and the thought of him walking away kickstarts my mouth.

"Wait!"

He freezes, his shoulders tense. I take a second to appreciate the man before me, the man who is the boy I once loved. Shit, still love if I'm being honest.

No. Not the time.

"Stay."

Flash lowers his head. "Why Jaci?" he asks and turns back around to face me. "Oh, right. Because you're the one who does the leaving."

I wince at his words. His bitter tone is such a stark contrast to what I'm used to from him. But then I remember that I don't know the man, not like I knew the boy. Wyatt wasn't bitter, he wasn't angry or mean. But Flash? I don't know him at all.

"That's what I thought," he snaps when I remain silent.

He turns on his heel and walks out of my office, slamming the door shut behind him. I collapse onto my chair and hold my head in my hands. As much as his reaction hurts, I know I deserve it. At least based on the information he has... which is nothing.

"What the hell happened?"

I lift my head and see Tina standing in front of my desk. Her expression softens as she rushes around to squat next to me.

"Hey, why the tears?"

Wiping my cheeks, I feel the wetness on my hands. I hadn't even realized I was crying.

"Jaci, talk to me," she pleads. "What happened? Flash burst in my office demanding to be transferred to another facility and then I come in here and you're crying. My imagination is—"

"Flash is Wyatt."

"Say what."

"Flash is Wyatt," I repeat. "Wyatt is Flash. They're the same person."

"I... I heard you. I just..." Tina shakes her head as if to clear it. "Wyatt? As in Wyatt King, the kid you were in love with in high school?"

"The boy who got me pregnant, the boy my parents hated, the one I was yanked away from... yeah. One and the same."

Tina lowers herself to her ass and crosses her legs. "Wow."

I huff out a humorless laugh. "Wow doesn't even begin to cover it."

"No, no it doesn't."

"So, what are you going to do?"

I groan. "I don't know. He's a patient, so I—"

"A patient who wants moved to a different rehab," she reminds me. "And even if he didn't, this is a huge conflict of interest. You can't work with him."

"I know, but..."

Tina narrows her eyes. "But what, Jaci?"

"I think I can help him."

"Seriously?" Tina stands and crosses her arms over her chest. It's not often she gets frustrated with me, but I always know when she does because she wears the same look she's sporting now. The one that screams *you're a fucking idiot*. "You don't even know this man. I highly doubt he's the same person you knew when you were sixteen. And it's a huge ethics violation for you to work with him."

What the hell am I supposed to say to that? She's right. I don't know Flash. But people don't change that much at their core, right? And as far as ethics go...

You have no leg to stand on with that one.

I rub my temples to try and stave off the elephant-sized headache forming. "I need to talk to him."

"And what are you going to say?"

"I don't know."

"Jaci, hun, I love you. You're not only my business partner, but my best friend." She leans forward to cup my cheeks. "And because of that, I worry that talking to him will only hurt you."

"And YGT," I add.

"Okay, yes, I worry about that too. One of us has to."

"Do you really think I would jeopardize all of our hard work, our facility?"

She straightens, and her arms fall to her sides. "Not on purpose, no. But the same can't be said about Flash. Or his club. I have no clue what they'll do if they get wind of this."

Shit. I hadn't considered that. Regardless of the consequences, I have to try. I can't ignore this, ignore him.

"Tina, just..." I blow out a breath. "Can I just talk to

him? Not as his therapist or even a representative of YGT. Just as Jaci. Please?"

Tina's head falls back, and she stares at the ceiling. When she looks at me again, her eyes are sad. "I'm not your boss, and even if I was, I can't tell you what to do on your own time. So, why don't you take the rest of the day off? Do..." She waves her hand. "... whatever it is you need to do."

I jump up and throw my arms around her. "Thank you."

"But..."

I lean back to look her in the eyes. "But what?"

"You can't treat him. You know that."

"I know."

"I'm going to have to honor his request and help him find another facility."

"Okay."

"And..."

"And what?" I ask, fearing she'll keep throwing out things just to stall.

"And as your best friend, I'm taking the rest of the day off too. "Something tells me you're going to need a shoulder when you're done with him."

That's not what I was expecting, and my muscles relax slightly. "Thank you."

"You're welcome." Tina grabs my hands and pulls me to my feet. "Now go, before I decide I'm going with you."

I throw my arms around her neck and give her a hug before heading toward the door.

"Jaci?"

I glance over my shoulder and look at her.

"You got this," she says with a smile.

Chapter Six

Maybe fate put us in each other's paths because that's exactly where we're supposed to be... together.

Flash

I pace the length of my room, my boots thudding on the tile floor in rhythm with my thundering heartbeat. Seeing Jaci again has always been top on my list of things to do before I die, but, deep down, I never thought it would actually happen. And certainly not while I'm at rehab for a cocaine addiction.

Fuck, I could go for a line right about now.

When I stormed into Tina's office and demanded to be moved to a different facility, she was shocked. No doubt she's more concerned about the money YGT will lose with my departure than she is about my rage. But she should be worried about my rage because it's burning holes through my entire body in order to break free.

On what has to be my hundredth pass across the room,

a faint knock sounds at the door, halting me in my tracks. I have to strain to hear it again, but it's there.

I storm to the door and yank it open. Jaci stands there with her eyes lowered, and she's fidgeting with her hands. Every second of pain I've experienced since that long ago Sunday threatens to douse my anger, but I maintain a firm hold on the fury.

"Can we talk?" she asks without lifting her gaze.

Goddammit! Why does her voice send me flying back in time?

I shouldn't invite her in, shouldn't *want* to, but the broken parts of me need to be near her for as long as possible, even if I'm mad as hell.

I step aside and sweep my arm wide. "Come on in."

Jaci hesitates for a moment but walks through the doorway. I slam the door behind her, shutting us inside for what is sure to be an explosive conversation. Spying my cut hanging over the back of the chair at the small desk, I move to grab it. After I put it on, I feel less exposed, more in control.

You're a damn liar! You don't feel anything but insanely out of control.

"Is that supposed to scare me?" she asks.

Jaci is finally looking at me, and I can decipher her expression. There's a hint of curiosity, maybe a bit of fear, and then there's a whole lot of... regret?

"No," I answer honestly.

She nods. "Good. Because you don't scare me."

Fury lashes at me like a whip. I stalk toward her, and her eyes widen. Gripping her arms, I back her into the wall and lean into her face.

"I should scare you," I snarl. "I should scare the fucking

shit out of you, Jaci, because I'm barely keeping a leash on my emotions."

My eyes drop to her throat, the slender column of flesh bobbing as she swallows. I shift a hand up to her neck and circle her throbbing pulse point with my thumb. Jaci shivers from the contact, and my cock jerks in my jeans.

"Fucking hell, Jaci," I groan.

"Wya—" She presses her lips into a thin line and inhales through her nose. "Flash, I... we need to talk."

Jaci flattens her palms against my chest and tries to push me away, but I don't budge. I should. I need to. But I can't. I'm completely and totally incapable of distancing myself from her.

"Fourteen fucking years." My grip tightens, and she whimpers. "Goddammit."

Her scent invades my senses, a mix of vanilla and pear that is somehow uniquely her. How the fuck am I supposed to stay mad at her when just being in her presence levels me?

"Flash," Jaci whispers. "Please."

I lean forward and bury my nose in the hair by her ear. "Please what?" I growl.

"T-talk. We n-need to talk."

I close my eyes and take one last deep breath, trying to get my suddenly raging hormones under control. Only when I'm confident I can focus on the conversation do I step back, releasing her as I do.

I force my thoughts to return to fourteen years ago, to the utter devastation I felt when I watched the security feed, when I saw the one word that sent me spiraling on that stupid piece of paper. The anger, the bitterness, the burning need to forget returns.

"What could we possibly have to talk about?" I ask, crossing my arms over my chest as I take a few steps back.

Jaci smoothes her shaking hands over the royal blue sweater hugging her curves, curves that weren't there the last time—

Stop!

She takes a deep breath and squares her shoulders. "I get that you're angry, but..." She begins to pace. "But... what the hell happened to you, Wyatt?"

"What happened to me? What the hell happened to me?" My voice rises as I repeat myself. "You fucking left!" I shout. "You left and never once looked back."

She stops pacing to stand in front of me, her eyes swirling fire. "Is that what you think? That I left you?"

"It's what happened. It was a normal Sunday, but when I showed up, you were gone. Hell, the whole family was."

"I didn't have a choice!" she yells. "My parents found out about—" She slams her mouth shut and inhales through her nose before continuing. "My parents didn't give me a choice."

"It's not like you fought it."

She glares at me. "What's that supposed to mean?"

"Aw, c'mon, Jaci." I throw my hands up. "I saw the video. Ya know, the security feed. I saw you packing a bag and it wasn't exactly like daddy dearest was holding a gun to your head."

Jaci's expression falls. "You saw that?"

"Yeah, I did." I smirk. "By the way, how's our kid doing? They're what, fourteen or so now?"

Her face pales as her body deflates and she stumbles back as if pushed. Her hand flies to her mouth, and tears spring to her eyes only to slip down her cheeks. It's not even close to the reaction I was expecting, and in the deepest recesses of my mind, I know I fucked up.

A ball of dread grows in the pit of my stomach, increasing in size like snow rolling down a hill. It gets so big that it no longer fits and turns to bile climbing up to my throat. I swallow it down.

"Jaci?"

She doesn't respond. She sways on her feet as she continues to stumble backward. Once, twice, three times until she hits the wall and slides down until she's on the floor.

I step forward, but she holds her hand out, silently demanding I stop. I do, for a moment, but then tentatively step forward again. Her silent crying erupts into gut-wrenching sobs when I kneel in front of her.

As pissed off as I am, knowing that I'm the cause of her anguish makes me feel like a giant asshole. She's the last person in the world I want to cause pain, even if she's the one who broke me.

"Jaci, talk to me."

She snorts through her tears, and I can't help but smile at that. My Jaci, the girl I loved with my whole being, is still in there somewhere. And the already broken parts of me shatter into millions of tiny pieces because the love I had for her then is still as deep now, still as all-consuming.

Reaching forward, I cup her cheek, and she leans into my touch. Her eyes are still brimming with tears, but she's coming back to herself, coming back to me.

And maybe that's the point. Maybe fate put us in each other's paths because that's exactly where we're supposed to be... together.

Maybe, maybe, maybe. So much uncertainty mixes with

the one and only certainty in my life, the opposing mindsets swirling together like the colors in marbled granite.

I know, unequivocally, that I love Jaci. Irrevocably so.

Always.

Forever.

No matter what.

And isn't that just a kick in the fucking junk?

I brush the tears off her cheek with my thumb and take a deep breath.

"Why don't you go back to the beginning and explain what happened?"

Chapter Seven

It's a damn good life. And then you showed up. Why the hell did you have to show up?

Jaci

The beginning.

He wants me to go back to the beginning. The beginning of what is the question. The beginning of my love for him? Or the beginning of my downfall? Or how about the beginning of the end of my life as I knew it? And then there's the beginning of my healing.

Oh, wait. That hasn't even started. Not really. I don't know that I'll ever heal.

"I don't know where to start."

Flash chuckles, and the sound washes over me like a calming balm. It slings me back to a simpler time, a happier time, a time when a certain boy and I had the world at our fingertips.

"Start at the be—"

"The beginning," I finish for him. "Easier said than done."

Flash removes his hand, and a stinging cold whips through me. I ignore it, knowing there needs to be some distance between us for this. If he's too close, I'm liable to take comfort that shouldn't be there. Because even though I didn't have a choice in anything as a teenager, he's right to be pissed. I never called, never tried to explain, never did a damn thing to make it right.

In my defense... well, there is no defense. Not really.

Flash stands and extends a hand to help me up. I take it, letting him tug me to my feet, but immediately move to sit in the chair across the room. His stare follows me, caresses me like a physical touch.

"First, you should know..." I avert my gaze to stare at the wall. This is hard. So goddamn hard. "There, uh... there is no kid."

I'm not looking at him, but it's not necessary for me to see Flash to feel the tension coiling his muscles. I'm as attuned to him now as I was when we were teenagers. That invisible thread that binds us together is still very present, and stronger than I remember.

"But I saw the paper," he argues, his tone laced with denial. "You were pregnant. I got you pregnant."

"You're right. I was. Until I wasn't."

"I don't understand. Did you miscarry?"

I shake my head, and fresh tears roll down my cheeks. "No. No, nothing like that." I finally meet his stare. My heart squeezes and breathing becomes unbearable. But I forge ahead. "My, uh, my parents..." I swallow past the lump in my throat, the one that's always there when I think about our child. "My parents forced me to have an abortion."

"What?" he snarls as he stalks toward me. "I don't think I heard you right."

Flash

My body deflates. I implore him with my gaze to understand, to let the words I'm saying sink in. "I had an abortion, Wyatt." His given name rolls off my tongue effortlessly. I know he doesn't want me to use it, but I can't help it, especially when talking about this. I swipe at my cheeks. "I didn't have a choice," I sob. "I wanted our baby. So damn bad. You have to believe me. I wouldn't have done it, I swear to you. I couldn't have done it. I want—"

He grabs my hand and yanks me up and into his chest. I collide with solid muscle, and strong arms encircle my waist, holding me tight.

"Stop," he snaps, although I don't think the heat in his tone is directed at me. "Just stop."

"But I need you to know," I mumble into his shirt. "I never would have gotten rid of our baby."

"Shhh," he soothes. "I believe you."

I rear back and level my crying eyes on his face. "You do?"

"Yeah, babe. I do."

Fresh tears fall at his use of the nickname he had for me when we were young. He always called me 'babe', whether he was being serious or silly. I'd forgotten how much I missed it.

"God, I love you."

The words are out of my mouth before my brain catches up. For a split second, I want to call them back, pluck them from the air like a child does a lightning bug. But there is no calling them back, no denying the truth in them.

Flash's expression shifts, becomes unreadable.

"I, uh… I'm sorry," I mumble, stepping out of his embrace. "I shouldn't have said that."

So much for not calling them back.

"Are you?" he asks. "Sorry?"

"Yes. No." I sigh. "I don't know. Should I be?"

"Did you mean it? Do you love me?"

I begin to pace again. "Of course I meant it. I loved you when we were sixteen and, fuck if I know why, but I love you still."

"Why?"

Seriously? Didn't I just say I didn't know why?

I stop in front of him, somewhat exasperated. His one-worded question is so simple, yet so complicated. I say the first thing that comes to mind.

"Because you're it for me. Forever."

His eyes soften at the old phrase, the one I uttered countless times before.

"Jesus." He thrusts a hand through his hair, then tugs on his beard. It's long, so much longer than the stubble from his youth. "What am I supposed to do with that?"

"I don't know. But I can't change how I feel. I never could where you're concerned. Just because I wasn't there with you, doesn't mean I forgot about you or that my feelings stopped. Despite the lengths my parents went to in order to force me to their way of thinking."

"I'm gonna fucking kill 'em," he seethes. His emotions are as all over the place as mine. "I'm gonna hunt them down and rip them apart from the inside out."

I arch a brow. "Really? That's your solution?"

"What else is there to do, Jaci? They took you from me, took our baby from us, and I'm supposed to just sit back and accept it?" He narrows his eyes, and suddenly, I witness the man, the danger lurking just beneath the surface. "How's that working for ya?"

He's got emotional roller coasters down to a science.

Indignation rises, replacing every ounce of sadness. "Pretty damn well!"

Flash

Flash huffs out a breath. "Right. And grass is purple."

"What do you want from me?" I cry.

"I want some honesty," he counters hotly. "All I want is some fucking honesty."

"Fine. You want honesty? Here ya go." I stomp close to him and stab a finger at his chest. "I was forced to have a part of me, a part of *us*, ripped from my body like it was nothing more than a skin tag. And then, because my parents wanted it done all hush hush and didn't even take me to a hospital or proper fucking clinic, the entire procedure was botched, making it impossible for me to ever have kids." I punch him with both my fists. "Oh, and then I tumbled so far down a goddamn hole of nothingness, numbing every single second of pain with pills, that I wasn't sure what was up and what was down and what was good or bad or even real."

I hammer his chest, over and over and over again until my knuckles hurt from the blows.

"I had no one, Wyatt! No fucking one! My parents shipped me off to a boarding school because they couldn't stand to look at me. They didn't even come to my graduation." I laugh, the sound maniacal. "They sent a card though. A generic dollar store card with a note that detailed how much of a disappointment I was to them. And then... oh, this is good. *Then*, they politely explained, in the note in the generic dollar store card, that I would be attending a college they chose, and I would major in political science so I could 'make something of myself'." I use air quotes around the phrase, and I swear even the action oozes sarcasm. "I called them to tell them to fuck off and guess what? They didn't even have the nerve to answer my call. I had to leave a voicemail."

I suck in air, ignoring the burn in my lungs from my

tirade. "I haven't heard from or spoken to them since." I tilt my head thoughtfully. "Which is a good thing, right? If I don't hear from them, they aren't controlling my life. And ya know what else, Wyatt?"

He stares at me, his eyes wide. "What?"

"I made something of myself. I pulled myself out of my addiction, on my own, graduated with honors, went to college—one I chose, by the way—and became a therapist. It might not be the life I envisioned when we were sixteen, but it's a good one." I start to lose steam, my energy flagging. "It's a damn good life. And then you showed up. Why the hell did you have to show up?"

"You're an addict?"

Oh. My. Fucking. God.

"That's what you're taking away from that? That I'm an addict?"

Flash shifts his weight from one foot to the other, seemingly uncomfortable all of a sudden. Good. Because this whole situation is un-fucking-comfortable.

"Ya know what?" I stomp toward the door and yank it open. "Forget it. It was great seeing you, Wyatt. Have a nice life."

I leave his room and run straight into Tina, who takes one look at me and wraps me in her arms.

"How much did you hear?" I ask.

"Enough."

"So all of it."

"Yeah," she confirms.

"Can you get him transferred to another facility?"

"Yeah."

"Thank you."

"You're welcome."

Flash

"Can we go get drunk?"
"Yeah."
"Will it numb the pain?"
"Afraid not."
"Didn't think so."

Chapter Eight

Even their violence comes from a place of love and loyalty.

Flash

"It's been three days."

I clench my hands at my sides as I hold my cell against my ear with my shoulder. After Jaci stormed out of my room, I called Fender to tell him the club can strip my patch. I can't do this. Not sober anyway.

"And it's too fucking hard," I bark.

"Bullshit," Fender snaps. "Several hours ago you were all in. Now you're just throwing in the towel and giving up your patch? What the hell happened?"

I heave a sigh. "Nothing happened. Turns out sober life just isn't for me." The lie comes easily.

"See, that's the thing. I'd be more inclined to believe that if I hadn't already received a call from that Tina chick," he says. "Wanna know what she had to say?"

My gut clenches with dread. I don't know what Tina knows, but I overheard her and Jaci talking after Jaci left, so

Flash

I know she likely has more information than even I did a few hours ago.

"Does it matter what she said?"

"Yeah, Flash, it matters. Tina said that you burst into her office and demanded a transfer to another rehab." Fender pauses to let that sink in. "So tell me, *brother*, why would you be asking to go to another rehab if all you really want to do is get high?"

I say nothing. What the fuck is there to say? Fender isn't stupid. He knows I'm lying. But I'm not ready to tell him the truth. Hell, I don't even know what the truth is anymore. I'm as confused now as I was the second I saw Jaci again.

"Ya know what?" Fender says, his tone calm, controlled. "Fine. You can come back, and we'll strip your patch. I'll send someone to pick you up in the morning."

A sigh escapes past my lips in relief even as my heart pounds in my chest. "Thank—"

Fender disconnects the call. I focus on the screen for a second, giving myself time to let reality catch up with me. I flop onto the mattress and fold my arms under my head. Staring at the ceiling, I think about what comes next.

After tomorrow, I won't have a home, or a family, anymore. As soon as my patch is stripped, I'll be as non-existent to the Soulless Kings as Santa Claus is to an adult. I won't have a job or any way to pay bills.

Bills. Fuck.

Being a patched member of Soulless Kings MC meant I had all the necessities provided to me. Sure, I'm the treasurer and paid bills for the club, but it wasn't with my own money. Money that I have no way of earning.

Quit with the pity party. You're better than this.

Am I? I'm not so sure about that. I grew up on the

wrong side of the tracks, and when I was old enough, I prospected for the club. A club that earns its money on the wrong side of the law. Maybe I'm as bad as Jaci's parents always thought.

Rolling to my side, I curl the pillow under my head. I might not know what comes after tomorrow, but it might not matter. Having my patch stripped isn't going to be easy. It's not like Fender's simply going to rip the thing from my cut. No, it's going to be bloody, violent, possibly... fatal.

But that's what I signed up for when I prospected. I knew that being a Soulless King was for life. Which means that tomorrow might be my last day on this Earth.

Is that what I want?

No.

Am I ready to die?

Fuck no.

But do I accept that, unless I bare my soul about Jaci, it's likely what will happen?

Yes.

* * *

"That didn't last long."

I toss my duffel into the bed of the truck before climbing into the passenger seat of Royal's truck. Why Fender sent him to pick me up, I don't know, but it's probably better this way. Facing any of the other officers would be torture right now.

The torture is coming.

"Just drive, prospect," I snap as I slam the door.

"Not a prospect, Flash."

Royal stomps on the gas, and the tires squeal as he roars out of the parking lot. Every fiber of my being wants to look back and see if Jaci is anywhere in sight, but I manage to ignore the impulse.

"Right. Sorry."

We ride in silence for a few minutes before Royal pulls over into the parking lot of a grocery store. He shoves the gear shift up, kills the engine, and twists in his seat to look at me.

"Are we really not gonna talk about this?" he asks.

"About what?"

The youngest patched Soulless King thrusts a hand through his hair and sighs. "The fact that I'm a rat," he snaps, his expression pinched, ashamed.

I turn and narrow my eyes at him. "Did you go to the po-po and give them info about the club?"

"No." Royal's tone is filled with confusion.

"Did you tell an outsider about the Nightmare Room or what happens there?"

He shakes his head. "You know I wouldn't do that."

"Did you call the—"

"Mother fucker, Flash!" he shouts as he punches the steering wheel. "Quit playing dumb."

"I'm just trying to figure out why you think what you did makes you a rat," I tell him. "Did you go to Fender because you were hoping to get me kicked out of the club?"

"Of course not," Royal scoffs. "I'd never do that."

"Why'd you do it then?"

"Because brother. You're family, blood or not, and I refuse to lose another family member to powder."

"You're not a rat, Royal. You're a damn good brother."

He shakes his head. "You're not mad?"

I huff out a laugh. "At you? No."

Royal sags with relief. "Oh thank God."

I turn back to face the windshield. "Look, it's not your

fault I'm an addict. It would be so easy to blame you for all of this, but..." I shrug. "The blame lies at my feet, not yours."

The cab of the truck grows silent. Royal faces forward and turns the key. I'm grateful for the reprieve, but it's short-lived because he just as quickly breaks the silence.

"You're not really giving up your patch, are you?"

"Yes, I am."

"But why?"

"Because it's easier than trying to get sober," I say absently, giving him the same line of bullshit I gave Fender.

"I'm not buyin' it."

"Not selling anything," I counter.

He nods slowly. "Okay. If that's the way you wanna play this." Royal reaches into his pocket. "Here, I got you this," he says as he opens his hand to reveal a small baggie of what appears like cocaine. "Figured you'd need it."

My eyes dart from his hand to his eyes and back again. It would be so damn easy to take what he's offering.

"Take it." He thrusts his hand closer to me.

"What are you doing?"

"I'm giving you what you need."

I remain still despite my demons clawing their way through my skin. My teeth ache from clenching my jaw, and Royal's stare is boring a hole into the side of my face like a laser beam.

"Yeah," he says and shoves the baggie back in his pocket. "That's what I thought."

Royal returns his focus forward and, after throwing the truck into gear, pulls out of the parking lot. He messes with the buttons on the steering wheel until Metallica blares through the speakers. I wish I could say the music drowns out my thoughts, but no such luck.

Did Fender put him up to that?
Where the fuck did he get the coke?
Would he have really let me snort it?
Ten minutes later, the music is cut off.
"Ready to tell me the truth?" he asks quietly.
"Fucking hell, you don't quit."
"Nope."

I run my hand over my beard, tugging slightly just to feel something other than uncertainty and annoyance. I'm fully expecting Royal to keep pushing me, so I'm surprised when he doesn't, when he just drives and waits.

"My life wasn't supposed to be like this," I finally say. I shift my eyes to see his reaction, but he doesn't have one. Not that I can tell, anyway. "My dad was a drunk who supplemented his alcohol intake with whatever drug he could get his hands on. Coke mostly."

"I'm sorry."

"Not your fault, kid." I glance out the passenger window and watch as the trees whiz by. "I didn't grow up with money, but I had what I needed. Roof, food, clothes. And a girlfriend who didn't give a shit about what I did or didn't have."

"Well, fuck."

I whip my head around and see his grip tighten on the wheel. "What?"

"This is about a bitch, isn't it?" he asks without looking at me.

Anger rises to the surface. "Her name's Jaci," I snarl.

"Got it. Jaci."

"Anyway, Jaci and I dated for a few years and when we were sixteen, her family just up and left."

"Damn, man."

"Long story short, it turns out she was pregnant, her

parents moved the second they found out, forced her to have an abortion, and I never saw her again." Again, I side-eye him to watch for a reaction. "Until yesterday."

Royal whips his head in my direction, and the truck swerves with his movement. I'm flung into the door, but he corrects his steering and straightens us up.

"Would you watch the goddamn road?"

"I am," he growls. "But you throw a twist like that at me, and... Never mind." He flexes his hands on the wheel. "So she's an addict too?"

Oh, and then I tumbled so far down a goddamn hole of nothingness, numbing every single second of pain with pills, that I wasn't sure what was up and what was down and what was good or bad or even real.

Jaci's words run through my mind. "Uh, yeah, I guess. But she's also the therapist at You Got This."

"Oh shit."

"Yeah."

Royal goes silent again. I imagine he's trying to put all the pieces together, trying to make them fit when it's impossible. Even with all of the information, nothing fits.

"Anyway, I couldn't stay at YGT."

"I'm guessing you didn't tell Fender any of this."

"No." I turn to glare at him. "And you better not either."

"Why?"

"Because it's my business, and I'm not ready to talk about it."

"But you just told me," he says unnecessarily.

"I did. And I'm trusting you to keep your fucking mouth shut. Think you can do that this time?"

Royal winces, and I know he can. And he will.

"Sure, Flash. I won't say anything."

I give a curt nod and return my attention to the scenery

out the passenger window. The rest of the drive to the clubhouse is quiet. Tension lingers in the small space, and my demons roar at the knowledge that Royal has what they need in his pocket, but I ignore it all.

Instead, I let images of Jaci fill my mind. Like a movie on fast forward, I replay every moment I've ever spent with her, starting with the first time I saw her walking down the hall in high school.

When we reach Soulless Kings' property, Royal slows the truck to a crawl as he comes to the gate. Parker, our latest prospect and former cop, is working security. He smiles at Royal, but his expression falls when he sees me.

"You're an idiot," he says as he leans in through the driver's side window.

"Nice to see you too, Parker," I mutter.

He focuses on Royal. "Fender said to have you bring him to the meeting room." Parker steps back and smacks the side of the door. "Good luck."

Royal drives through the gate once Parker opens it. I take in the property as if seeing it for the first time. Hell, it could very well be the *last* time. After he parks in front of the clubhouse, we both get out and head inside.

The normally rowdy main room is quiet. The TV is off, there are no pool balls clacking across the billiards table, and not a single man is sitting at the bar. Margo is there, though, in her usual bartending spot, and she levels me with a look of disappointment.

Get in line, Margo.

Standing in a line near the hallway are most of the ol' ladies. Charlie, Fender's better half, has her arms crossed over her chest while Alena, Holland, Luna, Riley, Lexi, Trinity, and Sylvia are sporting similar disappointed expressions.

"Ladies," I say when we reach them. "Nice to see I still warrant a welcoming committee."

"Fuck off, Flash," Charlie bites out as she shakes her head. "How can you do this? How can you so casually throw away everything that you are?"

"Trust me, Charlie," I begin. "There's nothing casual about this."

Royal snorts next to me, and I glare at him. He shrugs, but keeps his mouth shut.

"Ya know, addiction we can handle," Lexi, Squirrel's woman, says. "But leaving the club?" She shakes her head and tears well in her eyes.

"I don't get it," Riley, Joker's girl, says. "You love the Soulless Kings."

"I do," I confirm. "This isn't about the club. It's about me."

"Whatever," Holland, Piston's ol' lady gripes.

"Get him outta here," Luna, Riker's ol' lady and the president of the local Devil's Handmaidens MC chapter, snips.

Royal grabs my arm. Instinctually, I yank it out of his grip. The women part, like Moses parted the Red Sea, and let us through. When we reach the meeting room, Royal grabs me again.

"You know they're just hurt, right?" he asks quietly.

I glance over my shoulder at the girls and see them all huddled in a tight circle, banding together like the brothers do, like family.

"I know."

"They love you, Flash. We all do."

"I know."

Royal stares at me for a moment, seeming to silently ask me if I'm sure about this, silently begging me to reconsider.

Flash

"Let's get this over with," I say and open the door.

Standing around the table are my brothers. Fender, Joker, Piston, Riker, Trainwreck, Greaser, and Squirrel are all there. Burly, Pony, Chaser, and Curly are there as well. Shit, every single patched member is present. Which is exactly as it should be.

"All in favor of honoring Flash's wish to have his patch stripped, thump twice," Fender says, his eyes never leaving mine.

No one moves.

I twist slightly so I can pound the wall twice.

"It's not up to you," I tell them. "This is what I want."

"All opposed to honoring Flash's wish, thump once." Fender continues the vote.

Each of them thump the table once.

"And those of you who will go through the motions of stripping his patch regardless of whether or not you want to, thump twice."

Royal is the only brother who doesn't cast his vote.

So this is it. This is where my ride ends, with my brothers, my chosen family, stripping my patch because I'm asking them to. Even their violence comes from a place of love and loyalty.

"Nightmare Room," Fender orders. "Now!"

Chapter Nine

But I think you just might be the only person in the world who can stop this.

Jaci

"Are you sure about this?"

I keep my eyes on the road, so focused on my destination that it's difficult for me to carry on any type of conversation. Tina shifts in the passenger seat, bending her knee so she can face me.

"Are you, Jaci?" she asks again. "Because I'm not convinced it's the smartest move."

After I walked out on Flash yesterday, Tina and I practically bought out the liquor store and went back to my place. I got shit-faced drunk and woke up with a hangover that rivaled the one from my thirtieth birthday.

Was that really only a couple days ago?

But the hangover wasn't the only thing the alcohol gifted me with. No, it also provided me with some clarity. Doesn't make sense, I know, but there ya have it.

"I have to try, Tina," I tell her.

Flash

I have no idea where Flash and I go from here, if anywhere. What I do know is that I can help him. Maybe not in any official capacity, because, well, ethics. But I can be for him what Tina was for me through my addiction. A sounding board, a supporter, a cheerleader, a... friend.

"And if this blows up in your face?" she counters. "What if this sends you back to the pills?"

"It won't," I say with conviction.

I hope to God I'm not lying.

Tina's right. This could backfire, and I could seek solace in pills. But I have to believe that that isn't going to happen. It can't happen.

Tina points out the windshield. "Take a right at the next intersection," she instructs, giving me directions from the GPS on her cell.

"How much farther?"

"Little more than half an hour."

"Okay."

The remainder of the drive is quiet, except for Tina calling out directions. I go over what I want to say to Flash when I see him, play different scenarios out in my mind as some sort of one-sided dress rehearsal. It doesn't calm my nerves, but I'm certain nothing will.

When we reach the address—which wasn't exactly easy to find—I slow down and turn onto the gravel drive. To the left, there's what appears to be a guard shack, and a closed gate in front of us.

A man steps out of the shack, and he's wearing a leather vest—no, a cut according to that biker show—similar to the one Flash was wearing yesterday, so I know we're in the right place. I roll down my window and smile at him.

"I think you got turned around somewhere," he says.

I look past him at the road and turn to look the other

direction before beaming at him again. "Oh, no. I don't think so. This is the property of the Soulless Kings MC, right?"

"Who's asking?"

"Oh, um, my name's Jaci." I point to my passenger. "And this is Tina. We're here to see Flash."

"Nice to meet you." He grins, but it doesn't reach his eyes. They're as dark as the night and full of... resignation? "I'm Parker. I'm also the unlucky son of a bitch who gets to tell you to turn around and go home."

Tina leans across the center console. "Look, we just want to talk to Flash and then we'll leave. Promise."

"You misunderstand. I'm not doubting either of you, but Flash is... *indisposed* at the moment."

"What's that supposed to mean?" I snap, worry fraying the already ragged edges of my nerves.

"It means," he begins with what sounds like a very limited amount of patience. "That he can't come to the phone right now. Please leave a message at the tone, and he'll get back to you as soon as—"

Parker straightens and looks beyond the gate at the sound of a rumbling engine. A motorcycle comes into view a second later, and straddling the chrome beauty is a female with long flowing hair. Parker rushes to the shack and opens the gate. The woman stops the bike between my car and Parker.

"What's going on?" she asks him.

"They wanna see Flash," Parker tells her.

The woman looks at me and bends to also take in Tina. "Who are you?"

"I'm Jaci and this is Tina," I explain. "We work at You Got This Recovery."

"Charlie, I've got this," Parker says.

Flash

Charlie doesn't even acknowledge Parker's statement. "I'm Charlie," she tells us. "I'm Fender's wife."

"Fender, the president of Soulless Kings MC?" Tina asks.

"That's right," Charlie confirms. "What do you want with Flash?"

Well shit. I was hoping to get in and talk to him, not have to go through an inquisition for the opportunity.

"I'm the therapist at YGT," I begin. "I was hoping to talk with him and get him back into the program."

Charlie smirks. "Do you make house calls often?"

"No, we don't," Tina responds. "But this is a special case."

"Is that so?"

"Yes," I say. "You see, I knew Flash..." I shake my head. I really don't know what Flash has told anyone about me, if anything, and I don't want to divulge too much. But if it gets me in to see him, then I have to do it. Right? "We went to high school together," I hedge.

Charlie stiffens. "Then isn't it a conflict of interest to be here to convince him to go back to rehab? I mean, you can't treat him, right?"

"You're right," I admit. "I can't. Not as a therapist anyway. But I do think I can help him."

"Charlie, I don't think this is a good—"

"Shut up, prospect," Charlie snaps at Parker without looking away from me. "Don't make me regret this, Jaci." She rides around my vehicle so she's facing the now open gate. "Follow me."

When she takes off down the long drive, I don't hesitate. I press on the gas and follow. Tina looks over her shoulder as I look in the rearview mirror. Parker is standing there as the gate closes, and he's shaking his head.

What the fuck am I doing?

"I hope you know what you're doing," Tina says, her words mirroring my thoughts.

"Me too," I mutter under my breath. "Me too."

Charlie pulls up beside a building that I imagine is the clubhouse—thank you biker show—and shuts her motorcycle off. I park further away, as there are numerous other bikes parked in a line.

"Okay, I know I've been questioning you this whole time, but this is kinda exciting," Tina whispers as we get out of the car.

"Yeah, exciting."

"Oh, where's your sense of adventure?"

"And where was this positive attitude during the drive here?" I counter.

Charlie enters the building, and we follow. She gets to the center of the room before she stops and turns to face us.

"Before I take you any farther," she says. "I need to know one thing." I fidget with my hands, and Charlie arches a brow when she notices. "Shit. This is a bad idea." She starts to walk back toward the exit. "C'mon. You shouldn't be here."

"No, wait!"

She stops in her tracks and faces me again.

"I, um…" I take a deep breath. "Flash and I dated for a long time. And then circumstances outside of my control took me away from him."

"Go on," Charlie instructs when I pause.

I look at Tina, and she nods. "I loved him then, when I was sixteen." I swallow past the lump in my throat. "And I guess you could say I still do."

"You guess?"

"Look, I know you're probably trying to protect Flash,

but I'd really rather not air our dirty laundry. It's clear he's never mentioned me. Just know that I'm not here to make trouble."

"Jaci..." Charlie takes a few steps toward me. "It is Jaci, right?"

I nod. She knows it is. She's called me by my name already, and I didn't correct her.

"Trouble's already here, Jaci." Charlie tips her head back and inhales deeply. "Mother fucker!"

"Seriously?" Tina snaps as she steps toward Charlie, her hackles up in my defense. "I get that you don't know us, and maybe Flash never mentioned Jaci, but that doesn't give you license to be a bitch."

Charlie slowly lowers her head to glare at Tina. "Is that right?"

"Yes, dammit. Jaci is the sweetest, most genuine person on the planet, and I'll be damned if you make this harder on her." Tina takes another step forward, then another until she's less than a foot from the biker chick. "All she wants is five minutes with the man who's had a fucking death grip on her heart for the last fourteen years. I don't think that's too much to ask."

"Ya know what?" Charlie's face transforms as it lights up with a grin. "I like you." She turns to me. "And I like you. Most bitches run from me, but not you." She heaves a sigh. "Okay, c'mon."

Charlie walks around us, and Tina and I exchange a look. I shrug and turn to follow. We go down a long hallway, stopping at a steel door at the end.

"Before I open this door," Charlie begins. "You need to know that if you tell a soul about what you see today, the club will end you."

"Got it," Tina and I say in unison.

"I swear to fucking hell, I'm probably ending my sex life for the foreseeable future by taking you down there, so you better make the most of it."

"Uh, your sex life?" I ask.

"Yep. Fender is going to tan my ass for interrupting them, let alone bringing outsiders down to the Nightmare Room." Charlie tilts her head. "Hmm, maybe my sex life won't be ruined. I like it when he spanks me."

"The Nightmare Room?" Tina repeats.

"Brace yourself," Charlie says and then opens the door.

We follow her down a set of steps, but I don't see anything. Charlie opens a control panel and, after pressing a series of buttons, an image comes up on a screen to the right of another steel door.

I gasp at what the image reveals. Flash is hanging from the ceiling by two chains attached to his wrists. He's naked and bloody and being beaten by men with cuts, men that are supposed to be his family.

"It's not pretty," Charlie says. "Is it?"

"What the fuck are they doing?" I snap.

"Stripping him of his patch. It's what he wanted."

"But why?" I cry.

Charlie shrugs. "I don't know."

She presses another button, and the steel door slides open.

"But I think you just might be the only person in the world who can stop this."

Chapter Ten

Nothing changes... for now.

Flash

Pain travels up one side of my body and down the other. It's relentless in its pursuit to break me. But I refuse to let it.

"Keep going!" I shout when the blows stop.

Joker moves closer, his fist drawn back, but Fender sweeps his arm in front of him to stop him.

"He's had enough," Fender says.

"No," I bark. Blood coats my skin from my face to my toes. "Keep fucking going," I demand.

I don't know why I'm begging for this, for more torture, but I'm guessing it has something to do with wanting to go out like a man and not a pussy. I'm a Soulless King after all.

Not anymore.

Fender stares at me for a moment before lowering his arm. Joker takes advantage of the movement and lands a punch to my gut. I swing from the chains, and my shoulders almost pop out of socket.

"More," I say from behind clenched teeth.

I've been on the other side of stripping a patch. The process is brutal, but for some reason, they're taking it easy on me. Hell, Royal hasn't touched me at all. He's just standing against the wall with his arms crossed over his chest and his gaze averted.

"Fucking more!"

They all exchange looks, hesitant to do what I want. I focus on Fender, watching his expressions, his body language. He's a born leader and if he caves, the others will too. I just need him to give in to his instincts and fuck me up.

"Stop pussyfooting around, Prez," I snarl, blood dripping down my chin.

Prez must be the trigger word because Fender stiffens, and then all hell breaks loose.

"I'm not your fucking Prez," Fender roars.

Brother after brother, King after King lunges at me. Fists fly, boots connect with flesh, and pain ignites my nerve endings, penetrating every cell in my body.

My mind tries to blank it all out, tries to shut down. But I refuse to give in to that weakness. After several minutes of their assault, it becomes almost impossible to remain conscious. I fight it, fight the unrelenting need to pass out. My head hangs, my chin grazing my chest.

"Goddammit!" Piston shouts as he yanks my head up by my hair. "Fucking give in," he demands.

"N-no." I try to shake my head, but his grip is holding me still. "M-more."

I mentally brace myself for what I know will come if I

keep goading them. "C'mon," I plead, which sends me into a coughing fit. "Mo—"

"Stop it!"

Jaci?

My body finally gave in. That's the only explanation for why I'm hearing her voice in the Nightmare Room. I'm dead. They ended me, just like I asked them to.

"Tina, help me."

Jaci and Tina?

Arms wrap around my waist, and tits press against my thighs.

Tits?

Another set of arms joins the first, and I'm lifted slightly, which relieves the burning in my wrists and shoulders.

Maybe I'm not dead.

"Dammit, don't just stand there," Jaci cries. "Someone help us."

I try to lift my head, but it's impossible. My body is lifted and lowered, lifted and lowered, as if my weight is too great for whoever is holding me up.

"Here, let me."

Royal.

He hoists me up and off the chains. I'm dead weight in his arms so he maneuvers me so I'm over his shoulder like a damn flour sack, my bare ass pointed at the fucking ceiling.

"Royal, what are you doing?" Fender demands.

"What I should've done to begin with," Royal snaps. "I'm being a fucking Soulless King."

He carries me through the open doorway, and I catch sight of Charlie standing in the hall. She winks at me, but then her attention shifts at Fender's shout.

"Charlie, what the fuck?!"

"Don't take that tone with me," she snaps at her husband. Damn, she's got balls of steel.

"We'll talk about this later," he snarls at her.

Royal takes the stairs two at a time. The rich fucker is stronger than he looks.

"Where are you taking him?"

Jaci?

I forgot she was here.

Why is she here?

"Up to my room," Royal responds.

"You good if I monitor him there?" Gibson, the club doctor, asks.

"Yeah, no problem." Royal pauses on the last step. "I take it one of you ladies is Jaci?"

"I am."

"Good. You can come too. And so can your friend."

"Dammit, Royal," Fender snarls. "This isn't how things are done."

Royal says nothing as he continues walking. My body bounces over his shoulder, each jostle detonating an explosion of pain through me.

"Listen here," I hear Jaci growl. "This might not be how things are done, but I don't give a shit. You don't beat addiction out of an addict. What the fuck were you all thinking? He needs support. He needs his friends and his family. He fucking needs *you!*"

The corners of my mouth tip up. This is the Jaci I know, the Jaci I fell in love with as a teenager.

"Now, you've got two choices," she continues, a little calmer. "You can either..."

Her voice fades as I slip into the welcoming darkness of unconsciousness, my last thought that my girl can take it from here.

Flash

* * *

"It's not my job to make you understand."

My head throbs, and my mouth is as sticky as molasses.

"You're in my house bitch, so you better make it your job."

I try to open my mouth to tell Fender that he needs to watch his tone with Jaci, but I can't.

"Fender, stop." Charlie's plea filters into my subconscious. "You knew there was more to this whole patch-stripping thing, so don't act like a jackass now that you're getting some answers."

"I'm not getting answers," Fender barks.

"But you will," Jaci says sweetly. "As soon as he wakes up, I'm sure he'll fill you in."

Don't be so sure about that.

"N-no," I manage to croak. "I w-won't."

Small hands cup my face. "You're awake."

I open my mouth to respond, but nothing comes out.

"It's okay, just rest," Jaci says and smoothes my hair from my face. "You'll heal faster if you can rest."

My eyes flutter open, but I squeeze them shut at the invasion of light.

"Listen to her, Flash," Fender says, his tone full of resignation. Weight on the bed shifts, making me realize Fender was sitting on the edge of the mattress. "And yes, you will fill me in."

Footsteps thud on the floor as he leaves the room. Jaci's hands leave my face, and then a soft kiss is pressed to my cheek.

"He'll get over it, I promise." Charlie whispers in my ear. "And I like her, Flash. Don't fuck this up."

Charlie leaves behind her husband, and their bickering

filters through the air, quieter and quieter the further from the room they get.

"I've got you hooked up to IV meds."

My eyes fly open at Gibson's words. "No."

"Yes, Flash," he says flatly. "You need them."

"No."

"It's okay to take pain meds when you're hurting," Jaci says.

"No."

I lift my arm, ignoring the pain, and reach across my body to where the IV sticks out of my opposite hand. I yank out the thin tubing and toss it away as hard as I can. Which admittedly, isn't hard at all.

"Too hard to stay sober, huh?" Gibson taunts.

"F-fuck off," I mumble.

"Trust me, I plan to," he says with a chuckle. "Alena and I are gonna fuck like rabbits as soon as I'm done with you. Seems we both need to relieve some tension after all this bullshit."

"Do you guys always talk like this?" Tina asks, speaking up for the first time since I became conscious. I'm surprised she's still here. I don't know exactly how she fits in all of this.

"Pretty much," Royal responds.

"R-Royal," I say, and he steps up next to the bed. "Thanks."

His face hardens. "Don't thank me. I should've stopped it before it even started."

"Yes, you should have," Jaci snaps.

I shift my gaze to her. She looks like an avenging angel, her eyes tired but a bit wild and her body screaming *don't test me*. She's fucking gorgeous, and I'm... broken.

"It's okay," I tell her. "It's the way of things here."

"It's stupid."

"To an outsider, probably," I admit. "To a Soulless King, not at all." I reach for her, and she lets me link my fingers with hers. "I'm glad you're here."

"Are you?"

"Yeah."

"We still have a ton of shit to figure out and sort through."

I'm too tired to think about that now, so I nod. "Okay."

"I should probably head home soon," she says.

Tina rushes forward and wraps an arm around Jaci's shoulder. "Uh, no, you shouldn't. Stay here, make sure he's okay. I can cover the office and keep an eye on your place."

"What?" Jaci glances at her friend. "No. I can't miss work."

Tina smiles. "Yeah, Jaci, you can." She looks at me for a moment and then back at Jaci. "I think this has been a long time coming, don't you? Besides, you wanted to come here for a reason. Stay."

"You should listen to her," I add.

"You want me to stay?" Jaci asks.

"I want to know why you came in the first place." I shrug, and pain shoots through my neck. "But maybe we can get to it when I'm feeling better?"

Jaci seems to think about it for a moment, her mouth opening and closing several times, no doubt to offer objections. In the end, she settles on an answer I can live with.

"I'll stay, for now. But until we can actually talk, nothing has changed."

I pull my hand away and smirk at the way her face falls. "Okay. Nothing changes... for now."

Chapter Eleven

The past can't be changed. All you can do is take the information you have now and figure out how to move forward.

Jaci

"Are you heading home today?"

I down the shot Margo set in front of me ten minutes ago and slam the empty glass on the bar. I've been at the Soulless Kings clubhouse for a week now, and Flash is still recovering. But he's better, enough so that I can leave.

"I am," I tell Charlie.

"Have the two of you figured anything out?" she asks as she settles on the stool next to me.

"Do I look like we figured shit out?"

"Nope."

"I guess there's your answer."

"Then why are you leaving?"

"Because she's not cut out for this life."

Flash

Fender steps up behind Charlie and wraps his arms around her waist. He buries his head in her neck for a moment, and I turn away as jealousy slithers around me like a snake. These two didn't speak to each other for two days after the whole Nightmare Room thing, but she must have convinced him to see things her way because they showed up at the clubhouse on day three like nothing happened. It's all very... confusing.

"Oh, I don't know about that," Charlie says when Fender finally releases her. "I think she's tougher than she looks."

"She is," I snap. "And she's right fucking here."

"See, tough." Charlie beams a smile at Fender.

"And stupid." Fender moves to sit on the stool on my other side. I try to ignore him, but he spins me around, making it impossible. "Here's the deal, Jaci," he begins. "This is my club, which means we play by my rules. So, you either tell me what I want to know, or Flash is out. Which would really suck because he'd have to go through all that shit in the Nightmare Room again." He shrugs. "Since you stopped us the first time."

Fender, as well as a few of the others, have tried to get information out of me the entire time I've been here. And I've maintained that it's not only my story to tell. But this is the first time he's threatened to hurt Flash again, and I don't know what to do.

"Leave her alone."

I whip my head around and see Flash walking across the room. He's moving slowly, since he still refuses to take more than Tylenol for his pain, but he's up and that's a step in the right direction.

"Care to repeat that?" Fender's tone sounds lethal.

"You heard me."

"Your position in this club is still uncertain. Are you sure this is how you want to play this?"

Flash doesn't respond until he comes to a stop in front of Fender. "I'll tell you what you want to know," he says, surprising the hell out of me. And Fender, if his raised brows are any indication. "We both will. But not here."

"Fine." Fender stands. "My office, now."

Flash looks at me. "C'mon, Jaci. Might as well get this over with."

He grabs my hand and practically drags me along behind him as he follows Fender. I glance over my shoulder at Charlie.

"Are you coming?" I ask her.

"Do you want me to?"

Fuck yes! She's the only one I know who can keep her oaf of a biker man in line.

"Yes, please."

Charlie hops off the stool and rushes to catch up. Once we're all settled in Fender's office, silence ensues. I look from Fender to Charlie to Flash before throwing my hands up.

"Oh for fuck's sake, will someone say something?"

Fender focuses on Flash. "Why don't you start by telling me why you wanted to leave You Got This? Then we can go from there."

Flash lowers his head and strokes his beard. When he looks up, he reaches for my hand and grips it tightly, as if it anchors him somehow.

"Jaci and I dated in high school," he begins. "I hadn't seen her until I showed up for my therapy session."

"Okay, so it was a reunion. Still not understanding why that caused you to try throwing away your patch."

"Maybe if you let him talk, you'd understand," I snap, annoyed that he's still giving Flash a hard time.

Flash squeezes my hand reassuringly. "It's okay." He takes a deep breath and continues. "We didn't exactly part on the best of terms."

"Quit being cryptic," Fender orders.

I shoot to my feet, beyond capable of sitting back and letting Flash take the brunt of Fender's asshole attitude.

"You wanna know what he's hiding?" I demand as I step closer to Fender, who only stares at me with wide eyes. "He's not hiding shit about himself. He's keeping my secrets, my shame. And he's being damn polite about it if you ask me."

"All he had—"

"I'm not finished."

"I really, really like her," Charlie says from her position next to Fender.

"Thank you," I say without looking away from her man. "What Flash isn't saying is that my parents found out he knocked me up. They made me move, hired a less than stellar doctor to perform an abortion, which was botched, by the way. And then they shipped me off to boarding school. I turned to drugs but am better now." I take a deep breath and swallow past the pain this always brings. "And Flash didn't know any of this until last week. What he did know was that he loved me, and I left. He turned to drugs and wants to get better now. So, please, *Mr. President*, tell me what part of that he should have told you. Because from where I'm standing, he's barely had time to digest the information he *just* learned."

"I..." Fender shifts his gaze beyond me. "Is this true, brother?"

"For the most part, yes," Flash says as he stands and moves close to me.

"And you were willing to keep all of this to yourself and give up your patch?"

"Yes."

"Why?" Fender asks, and for the first time since I met him, he seems genuinely interested in an answer.

"Because everything I thought I knew was wrong." Flash shrugs. "Shame, fear, anger, sadness... name any emotion, and I'm sure it ties into my reasoning somehow."

"You know you could have talked to me."

"And say what? 'Hey, Prez, I'm addicted to coke, but don't worry because it doesn't cloud my judgment'," Flash says sarcastically. "Or how about 'Yo, bro, I'm an addict who only uses to forget the love of his life'. I'm an addict, Fender. We hide shit."

"Do the whys really matter?" I ask. "The past can't be changed. All you can do is take the information you have now and figure out how to move forward."

Fender's eyes dart from me to Flash and back again. And then he looks at Charlie, who bumps her shoulder into his side and grins.

"I don't think she heard that," Charlie says.

"Heard what?"

"Your own words," Fender responds before Charlie can. "You didn't hear your own words."

"Okay?" The word comes out more like a question.

"Flash, brother, you've still got a patch. None of the others wanted things to go down the way they did anyway. But you need treatment. We can discuss what that looks like after you take a few more days to heal." He turns to me. "And you."

"Me?"

Flash

"Yes, you." Fender swings a finger between me and Flash. "You both need to do exactly what you just said. Take the information you have now and figure out how to move forward."

Well, shit.

Chapter Twelve

I told her that Wyatt died a long time ago, but it seems I was wrong. He's still very much alive for her.

Flash

"I guess I'll get going."

I release the breath I was holding, grateful for Jaci breaking the deafening silence. After Fender and Charlie left us alone, it's been too quiet, too awkward. It seems we're good at defending one another, at barreling through the details of our connection to others, but we fucking suck at talking to each other.

Jaci stares at me, her penetrating gaze seeming to burn a hole clear through to my soul. Is she waiting for me to speak? What does she want me to say? Shit, what do *I* want to say?

"Don't go," I blurt.

"Give me a reason to stay."

One thought springs to my head, proving how fucked

up I really am. "Don't ask for things you're not prepared for."

This isn't the time, and definitely not the place, but my raging desire doesn't give a damn. I want her. I will always want her, no matter how tense and awkward things are between us.

Her pupils dilate, and her cheeks flush an apple red. The pulse point in her throat jumps, and my dick springs to life in my sweats. I take a step toward her.

"Do you have any idea what you do to me?" I growl as I force myself to keep my hands at my sides.

Jaci shakes her head, but when I glance down at myself, her gaze follows.

"Wicked things, Jaci. You do wicked things to me."

I take another step forward and, with my finger, lift her head up so she can see the heat in my eyes.

"It's been so long since I tasted you," I murmur. Leaning forward, I inhale her scent. "Vanilla and pear. It's always vanilla and pear." Acting without thought, I touch the tip of my tongue to the shell of her ear. "I wonder, do you still taste like everything that's good in the world mixed with a hint of delicious sin?"

Jaci whimpers.

"Do you still need me to give you a reason to stay?"

When she nods, I move to seal my mouth over hers. She's hesitant for a second, but as soon as I drag my tongue across the seam of her lips, she melts into me.

Jaci's arms go around my neck, and I smooth my hand down her side, over her hip, and lift her leg. She jumps so that she's straddling me. Pain flares at the sudden jolt, but it disappears just as quickly under the inferno of lust coursing through my veins.

I turn with her in my arms and back her into the door. I

slant my head to deepen our kiss. My nerve endings spark and sizzle, ignite and burn with every second our bodies are pressed together.

Jaci uses the door as leverage to thrust her hips forward, and my cock hardens to a painful degree. But it's the kind of pain that men have been craving and seeking since the dawn of time. Her hands tug at my hair before she drags her nails down my cheeks and claws at my t-shirt covered chest.

I hold her up with one hand while I yank the neck of her shirt down to bare as much of her as possible. Cupping her tit, I groan against her lips. She moans as my thumb grazes her nipple, bringing it to a hard peak.

Jaci's body jerks when there's a hard bang on the door.

"I'm the only person who fucks in there," Fender calls through the barrier. There's laughter in his tone, but I don't doubt for a minute that he's serious.

Jaci turns her head, breaking our lip-locked assault on each other, and the loss of that connection is like a bucket of water to my need.

"No one is fucking," she shouts.

Fender's chuckle is muffled by the door. "Uh-huh."

Jaci bangs her head against the wood, and I can't stop the huff of laughter that barrels out of me.

"Welcome to my world."

She narrows her eyes on me. "I'm not sure how I feel about your world."

I slowly lower her to her feet, and the drag of her body down mine is pure torture. After adjusting myself, I move back to put some distance between us. Otherwise, I'm going to shove my pants down and bang her into next week.

Jaci straightens her shirt to cover herself back up, and I turn away.

"This doesn't change anything, does it?" she asks, her tone soft.

I whirl around and move to cage her in, my hands flattened on the drywall on either side of her head. "It changes everything."

Doesn't it?

Jaci pushes me and ducks under my arm to walk across the room. "Flash, it doesn't. It can't."

Scrubbing my hands over my face, I take several deep breaths and try to ignore the bitterness creeping up my throat.

"Why not?"

"Because," she cries as she throws her hands up. She does that a lot, and it's not something I remember her doing when she was younger. She was much more agreeable then. I miss that. "For starters, we can't ignore the last fourteen years. And then there's the fact that you're an addict who needs treatment. Relationships are strongly discouraged during recovery."

I smirk. "Give me more of that, of you, and I won't need any drugs."

Jaci scoffs. "You can't trade one addiction for another. That's not how it works."

"Then tell me, how does it work? How are we supposed to move forward?"

"Well..." She starts to pace, her expression morphing from one emotion to another so quickly, I'd miss the shift if I weren't paying attention, if I wasn't so attuned to everything about her. "This is why I came here last week, to talk about your options."

"Options?"

"Yes, options. We both know you can't come back to

You Got This. I'm the primary therapist there and, as we've established, it's ethically wrong for me to treat you."

"Right."

"One option is to admit yourself to another rehab facility and work through the program. Professionally speaking, I have to acknowledge that this is probably the best option."

"I don't want your professional opinion," I tell her.

"Okay. Then my personal opinion, and option two, is that I still work with you, but not in any capacity related to my position at YGT. I can't compromise my career, nor will I. I've worked too hard to overcome my own addiction and build a life for myself."

"I don't want you to compromise any of it. Not for me."

"See, that's just it, Flash." She stops pacing to face me. "If ever anyone could make me compromise things, it's you. It's always *been* you and will always *be* you."

"Good to know." I move toward her, leaving only inches of space between us. "So, how would you help me in option two?"

"I'd be here for you, with you. I haven't seen you use anything for the last week, which tells me that your addiction doesn't rule your life. You have some control over it. But I'm not stupid enough to think you haven't wanted to use, or that you haven't craved the high."

"You're right about that," I huff out.

"So we'd take it day by day. You can talk to me, call me when the cravings hit. We can go to NA meetings, which, if I'm being honest, would be beneficial for both of us. I'd be your friend, Flash." Jaci tilts her head as if to study me. "I used to be the person in your life who could help you through anything. Let me be that person again."

"That all sounds great, but…"

"But what?"

"I don't know how to just shut off my feelings or forget about you leaving and what your parents did."

"I'm not asking you to shut it off or forget. But maybe Fender is right about me heeding my own words." Jaci shrugs. "We can't change the past. Trust me, I would if I could. But we can try to move forward with the information we have now."

I want to move forward, slay my dragons and forget the past. But how am I supposed to do that when, despite everything that's happened, she's a huge part of that past? I don't want to forget it all... just the bad parts. Because with Jaci, it wasn't all bad.

Can I forget that my world was upended when I found her house empty?

Fuck no.

Can I forgive her parents for their role in my downfall?

Fuck no.

But can I try to work through the pain I've suffered because of it?

Yeah, I can try.

Do I want Jaci to be a part of my journey through the dark?

Yes.

Is there a part of me that's hoping we can move forward together, as a team like we used to?

Fuck. Yes.

What if it doesn't work? What if she realizes I'm not the person she thinks she loves? What if she leaves again? What if I spiral into a dark pit I'm incapable of climbing out of? What if—

"Flash?"

"Yeah?"

"This won't work if you don't talk to me. I can see in your eyes that you're lost in a maze of doubt."

I shake my head, but when she quirks a brow, I stop. "Just thinking about all the what ifs," I admit.

"Okay." She bobs her head. "Let's talk about that."

"I don't know how."

Jaci grabs my hand and pulls me toward the couch. We both sit, me facing forward and her with her leg tucked under her so she can see me.

"Are you worried about going to another rehab?"

"No."

My response is immediate. There is no part of me that's contemplating another facility. I know which option I'm going to choose, despite the unanswered questions plaguing me. But that's the problem: the questions.

"Okay, so you're going with option two?"

"Yes."

"What has you worried about that?"

"Everything," I say with a sigh. "Every goddamn thing, Jaci."

Again, she lifts my hand in hers. "Wyatt, look at me."

The sound of my name coming from her lips almost levels me. I told her that Wyatt died a long time ago, but it seems I was wrong. He's still very much alive for her.

I twist on the couch, ignoring the ache in my ribs, and mirror her position.

"Do you trust me?"

I shouldn't. I've spent so much time and energy on all the reasons I shouldn't trust her.

And it was all a lie. She didn't leave, not by choice. She didn't keep your child from you.

I shouldn't, but I do trust her. God help me, I trust her. And that terrifies me.

"Yeah, I trust you."

Jaci tugs my hand and places it over her heart.

"Do you feel that?"

Her heart is beating wildly, erratically, just like mine.

"Yes."

"No matter what you thought, or where I was, or how numb I made myself..." Tears spring to her eyes. "No matter what happens, it always beats for you. Always."

I grab her free hand and flatten it against my chest. "Same. No amount of coke or alcohol or rage numbed me enough to stop feeling this, feeling you."

"Let me be your person again."

Her plea sends my heartbeat into overdrive, fear and hope fueling the adrenaline pumping through me.

"Okay."

"One day at a time."

"Okay."

We sit there, both soaking in the other's heartbeat, absorbing the thumping like we need it in sync to survive.

"Can I tell you something?" she asks.

"Anything."

"I'm scared too."

Chapter Thirteen

In a dark basement in Portland, Oregon...

"Are you sure?"

I roll my eyes at the question. I've been reporting to the man for almost thirteen years and every time we talk, he asks the same thing. I don't like being doubted, but he doesn't pay me to like him or anything he does. He pays me to do a job.

"I'm sure, Sir." Calling him 'Sir' goes against my nature, but I have a role to play where he's concerned. A role I'm very good at. I stare at the blinking red dot on my computer screen, the one that hasn't moved for days. "She's been there for a week."

"What's she doing there?"

"You pay me to keep tabs on her whereabouts, Sir," I remind him. "I don't dig into her reasoning for being at a certain location."

Lifting one of the many pens scattered across my flimsy desk, I flip it end over end between my fingers. When I was hired, it was for a very specific purpose, one that has never changed. If he wants to switch things up now, we need to discuss my... *fees*.

"What do you know about this, this, *biker* gang?" he stutters indignantly.

"What are you prepared to pay me for that information?" I counter.

"I pay you more than enough already."

"Yes, you do... to keep tabs on Jaci's location."

A rumble comes through the line, and it's all I can do not to laugh at the man.

"How much more do you want?"

"That depends."

"Dammit, Jerry. How much?"

"What information do you want me to ascertain? Tell me that, and I can give you a quote."

It took me a while to figure it out, but he responds better to a professional tone. The problem is, I'm the furthest thing from a professional. I just happen to be a damn good actor. I've had to be in order to stay alive over the years.

"I want to know why she's there," he snaps. "I want to know why she hasn't been to work in a week. I want to know everything!"

I whistle. "That's gonna cost you."

"How. Much?"

"Another ten grand a month."

"I already pay you five grand."

"And if you want me to do more, you have to pay more... Sir."

"Fine. Another ten thousand." His agreement is music to my ears. "Now find me everything you can on the Soulless Kings. Find out why Jaci is there."

"It will be my pleasure."

The line goes dead, and I let out the laughter I was

holding in. Mother fucker thinks he hired an idiot. I might not have a college education, but I'm no dummy.

I scroll through my contacts until I come to the one I need. I tap the screen and then put the call on speaker.

"Why are you calling me?"

"Parker, my man, how long has it been?"

Chapter Fourteen

Numb. I want to be numb. So goddamn numb.

Flash

"All in favor of Jaci staying here to work with Flash, thump twice."

Every brother in the room pounds the table.

As soon as I agreed to work with Jaci, outside of a facility, we talked to Fender about it. He seemed to think it was a good idea and called church so it could be put to a vote.

"Good," Fender says. "Flash, for the next month, you will hand over your treasurer duties to Curly. He's already the secretary, so at least we know he'll keep good records for you. We'll re-evaluate after the thirty days and go from there."

"Sure thing, Prez."

I don't like having someone else responsible for my job, but I understand it. I might still have a patch, but the trust the club had for me was broken, and I need to put it back together again.

"Since this session was unscheduled, I won't keep you much longer." Fender turns to Greaser. "Everything still ready for tonight?"

Greaser nods. "We ride out at eight, meet with the buyer at nine. If all goes well, we should roll back in by eleven."

"Do you need me for anything?" Fender asks.

"Nah, Prez, we got it covered."

"Go—"

All heads turn toward the door at the knock that interrupts our president.

"Who the fuck is it?" he demands.

"Parker, Prez."

"Prospects aren't allowed in church," Joker barks. "And they definitely shouldn't fucking interrupt."

"Understood," Parker calls through the closed door. "But we've got a problem, and it can't wait."

"Come in," Fender commands.

Parker opens the door and slams it behind him. He strides to the head of the table to stand next to Fender.

"Well, Prospect, what is it?" Piston asks when Parker doesn't say anything.

"I just got a call from an old contact," Parker begins. "Jerry was an informant for me over the years. He's got his hands in all sorts of underground pots, and our relationship was mutually beneficial. He gave me information on anything I needed, and he stayed out of prison."

"This concerns the Soulless Kings because…"

"One of Jerry's specialties is tracking people. He likes to think of himself as some sort of vigilante private investigator." Parker shrugs. "I never gave a shit what he called himself, as long as the information he gave me was accurate."

Flash

"Get to the point, Prospect," Riker spits out.

"I am," Parker assures us. "Anyway, he called and filled me in on a client he's had for a little over a decade." Parker turns to me and his jaw tics. "Does the name Stanley Stine mean anything to you?"

I shove up from my chair, and it crashes to the floor behind me. "What the fuck does that bastard have to do with the call you got?" I ask.

"It seems Stanley hired Jerry to keep tabs on Jaci."

"Who's Stanley?" Fender asks.

I clench and unclench my hands. "He's Jaci's father."

"Wait a second." Fender holds his hand up. "Her dad, the same one who forced her to have an abortion, has been keeping tabs on her? For how long? And why?"

"Jerry was hired thirteen years ago," Parker explains. "According to him, he was only tasked with knowing her location at all times. And he's damn good because he knew she's been here for the last week."

"How?"

"Like I said, he's good."

"In other words, he wouldn't divulge any trade secrets?" Gibson says.

"No, he wouldn't," Parker admits. "Not that he needs to. It's not too hard to track people these days."

"No, it isn't," Squirrel, our tech guru, says.

"Okay, so he knows she's here," Fender begins. "Why did he call you, Parker?"

"He heard through the grapevine that I'd quit being a cop, that I tied in with the club." Parker looks from Fender to me and back again. "He was giving Mr. Stine his usual monthly report, and Mr. Stine wasn't too happy. He asked Jerry to learn everything he could about the club. Jerry, in turn, called me. He knows I have information that could put him away for a very long time. He's a criminal, but not a stupid one."

"What does he want for telling you all of this?" I ask because no one does something for nothing.

"What do you think?" Parker counters, his expression glum.

"How much does he want?"

"Well, that depends. If we want him to simply not give Mr. Stine any information, twenty-five thousand. If we want him to feed Mr. Stine specific information, fifty thousand."

I pound the table with both fists. "Fifty grand?!"

"Hold up," Fender says. "He's willing to give Mr. Stine whatever we tell him to?"

"Yes."

"This could be a good thing," Joker adds. "It gives us control over the situation."

"No," I seethe. "Nothing good ever comes from the Stines. They're rich fuckers who will stop at nothing to get Jaci to fall in line. She's managed to get her parents out of her life. We're not dealing with them."

"It doesn't sound like they're as out of her life as she thinks," Piston says. I glare at my VP. "Besides, it's not up to you. The man wants information on the club, which means it needs to go to a vote."

My stomach churns like choppy ocean waters in a hurricane. I don't like this. I finally have Jaci back, albeit barely, and her parents jump out of the shadows.

An image of her father standing behind Jaci as she packs her suitcases flashes in my mind. A glimpse of Jaci lying on a bed, writhing in pain as our baby is taken from her, flickers into my consciousness. A snippet of Jaci swallowing pill after pill to escape the hounds of hell concludes my mental movie.

Numb. I want to be numb. So goddamn numb.

"Flash?"

Fender's voice penetrates the fog surrounding me. I turn to look at him.

"Is this going to be a problem?" he asks.

The words he doesn't voice give me pause.

"I don't know," I answer honestly.

And I hate that weakness, hate that my first thought is to go get high and numb the fury.

Rather than continue down that line of questioning, Fender glances at Parker. "Is there anything else you can tell us?"

"Just that Jerry wants an answer within forty-eight hours."

"And we'll have one. You can go."

"Prez, you should know, I trust Jerry," Parker says. "I don't expect you to understand that, but it's fact. And it matters."

"Noted."

Parker nods curtly and then leaves the room. As soon as the door closes, I lose my shit.

"I'll fucking kill them, Prez," I snarl. "I swear on all that's holy, I will hunt the Stines down and end their miserable, goddamn lives."

"All in favor of using Jerry to our advantage, thump twice," Fender calls for a vote, completely ignoring my threat.

I'm the only one not in favor.

Fender focuses on me. "Flash, you need to go find Jaci and fill her in," he orders. "And don't even think about seeking out a dealer because I'll be drug testing you at random times."

"Prez, you can't do this."

"I can, and I will," he insists. "I refuse to sit back and watch you kill yourself because you can't handle shit life throws at you. The Stines are just like every other monster we've come up against. We'll handle them, and we'll do it as a club, as a family." He crosses his arms over his chest. "Understood?"

"No," I snap. "I don't fucking understand. But..."

Son of a fucking bitch!

"... Understood."

Chapter Fifteen

I don't like being told what to do.

Jaci

"Stop worrying."

I cram more clothes into my bag before going to my bathroom and grabbing my toiletries. I've never been a fan of packing to go anywhere, but this time is different. Because deep down, way deep in my soul, there's a part of me begging for it to be the last time.

"I can't help it," I tell Tina, bracing my cell against my ear with my shoulder. "It's what I do."

She chuckles. "I know. But I've already hired a second therapist, so we're covered at YGT."

"You did?"

Is she replacing me? What if this therapist is better? Why wouldn't she include me in that decision? What if I—

"Stop it," Tina snaps. "I can practically hear your screaming thoughts from across town."

"I'm not quitting my job, ya know?"

"Jaci, honey, I never said you were. Never thought you were, either. But this is an opportunity that doesn't come along for everybody. You've got the love of your life back, and he needs you."

"Who said he's the love of my life?"

"Seriously? You did," she cries. "You've said it over and over and over again since I met you. Every time I held your hair while you threw up pills, you said it. Every time you cried, you said it. Every time you drank, you said it. Every time you denied it, you said it."

"Point made," I grumble.

"I'm not taking your job away from you," she continues. "I'm just making sure you have the time to do what you need to do to be happy. I know we're business partners, but we're best friends first, and all I want is for you to be happy, Jaci."

"What did I do to deserve a friend like you?"

"That goes both ways."

I throw my now too-full duffel over my shoulder and carry it out into the living room. After dropping it on the couch, I take one last pass through my home to make sure I'm not forgetting anything.

You can come back if you need to. Stop stalling.

"Hey, I meant to ask," I state. "How's Summer doing?"

"Really well, actually. Her parents come this weekend for a family session, so we'll see how that goes."

"Don't let them railroad her, Tina. Make sure the new therapist doesn't let them run the session because that will set her back more than—"

"This isn't my first rodeo, Jaci."

"I know. It's just..."

"Her parents remind you of yours," she finishes for me.

"So much," I groan.

"Jaci, are you okay? I mean, you're not thinking about old habits, are you?"

"No, no." I shake my head even though she can't see me. "Nothing like that."

"Good. Now, I know you're packed and ready to go, so why aren't you leaving?"

"What if this is a huge mistake?" I ask, voicing my fears. "What if we can never move past, well, our past?"

"What if you can?"

"Right. Okay." I take a deep breath as I turn off the last of the lights. "I can do this."

"You got this."

"I got this."

"Second chances, Jaci. They don't come around every day. Just roll with it, okay?"

"Roll with it," I repeat.

"And call me any time," she urges. "I mean it. You need me, you call."

"I will," I assure her. "You're acting like I'm leaving the country."

"I'm used to seeing you pretty much every day. I'm going to miss you. Sue me."

My phone vibrates with a notification, and I pull it away from my ear to look at the screen.

Flash: You need to get back to the clubhouse.

"You still there?"

"Oh, yeah, sorry. Flash just text me."

"And?"

"He said I need to get to the clubhouse." I scoop up my duffel and head out the door, locking it behind me. "What if he relapsed? Why do I need to get there? What if—"

"Oh my God, stop," she snaps, but there's no heat in her tone. "Text him back or call him and find out. Don't create trouble where there is none."

"Right." I throw my bag in the back of my car and then get in the driver's seat. "I'll call you later. Love ya."

"Talk to you later. Lo—"

I disconnect the call with a mental note to apologize later for cutting her off. After pulling up my texts, I type in a quick response to Flash.

Me: What's going on? Are you okay?

Three dots appear almost instantly, and I chew on my bottom lip as I wait for his response.

Flash: I'm fine.

And that tells me absolutely nothing.
Men!

Me: Leaving my place now. I need to swing by the store and grab a few things, but I'll be there soon.

Flash: Come straight here. We can go back out to the store later.

Me: It won't take me that long.

Flash: Straight here, Jaci.

I toss my phone on the passenger seat without responding. If he thinks this is how things are going to go between us, he better think again. I don't like being told what to do. He should know that.

And yet, as I drive, I pass store after store, anxious to get to the clubhouse. I find myself checking my rearview mirror at every turn, something in Flash's demand to go straight there triggering a nagging worry.

At one point, I spot a black sedan behind me, and my fight or flight response kicks in. I make several unnecessary turns, even though the car doesn't even follow the first one.

"You're fine," I mutter to myself. "You're being ridiculous."

The hour-long drive turns into an hour and a half. There were several suspicious vehicles, and no amount of mental pep talks curb my panic.

When I reach the clubhouse, there's a prospect manning the gate, but I can't remember his name. It doesn't matter though, because he waves me right through.

After parking my car at the side of the clubhouse, where Flash instructed me to before I left earlier, I carry my duffel inside. Charlie and a few of the other ol' ladies are sitting at a table in the main room, and when she spots me, she points to the stairs.

"He's waiting for you," she says.

"Thanks," I call over my shoulder as I race up the steps.

The door to his room is shut. I consider knocking, but don't bother. He told me that I needed to think of the clubhouse as my home, so I'm going to trust that he meant it.

I turn the knob and push the door open. Anger surges to the surface even as my feet become rooted to the floor.

Flash's head whips to the side at my entrance, and his eyes widen.

"Jaci, let me explain," he says as he takes a step toward me.

Oh, he better explain. Because finding him standing in front of his dresser, a perfectly neat line of white powder across the top, isn't at all what I was expecting.

Chapter Sixteen

Her words hold a level of truth that's undeniable. And her fear is real, so goddamn real that it penetrates and meshes with my own emotions.

Flash

The look of disappointment and shock on Jaci's face guts me.

"This isn't what it looks like," I say as I rush toward her.

"Not real clear on how that's possible."

When I reach for her, she backs away. Her reaction irks me. It really isn't what it looks like, but I'm an addict. What did she expect?

"Where'd you even get it?" she asks.

"It was in a drawer."

"A drawer?"

I thrust a hand through my hair and then my beard. "Yes, a damn drawer." Jaci stares at me like I have two heads. "What?" I bark.

She closes her eyes and shakes her head. "Let's back up and start over," she suggests. "Tell me what happened."

"What's the point? You've already made up—"

"Wyatt, stop!" Jaci shouts. "Just stop." Some of the tension in her shoulders eases. "I'm sorry. I shouldn't have jumped to conclusions."

"Yeah, Jaci, you should've."

"Huh?"

"Your conclusions were right. I was gonna snort it." I hold my thumb and index finger centimeters apart for her to see. "I was this close."

"Why?"

"Because you were late and not answering your phone, and I was freaking out," I snap.

She reaches into her pocket and pulls out her cell. As she glances at the screen, her face falls. "I didn't even know you called. I threw my phone on the passenger seat and the volume wasn't on, so I didn't know you called."

"You didn't..." I take a deep breath. "The volume was off on your cell?"

"Yes, it was."

"Oh."

"So you got freaked out and then what?"

I think that's pretty clear.

"I, uh... well, I was..." Why is this so hard? "I was cleaning out a couple drawers for you, okay? And I must have had some of my stash left. I tried to ignore it, but then you didn't answer your phone, and I started to panic that you were ignoring me and not gonna come back. I thought it was going to be like before." I nod at the line of coke. "And that's how I deal. So, yeah... that's what happened."

"You were making space for me?"

"I was."

Flash

"But I thought I'd be staying in a room of my own."

Aw, that's cute.

I stalk toward her and grip her biceps. "No, you're not. If you're here, you're with me. I'll sleep on the floor if that makes you feel better, but you're not sleeping in a different room. I'm not going to wake up some morning and think that everything is fucking peachy only to find you gone."

Jaci lifts her arms, which forces my hands to fall away. "I will not just up and leave. I promise you that."

"Don't make promises you can't keep."

"Wyatt, I will not leave you, not permanently, unless it's something we talk about first. You weren't the only one hurt by my family moving. I know what that pain feels like, and I'll never, *ever,* intentionally make you feel that again."

I want to believe her, I really do. But it's so fucking hard.

"Trust," she says. "We both have to learn to trust."

I nod absently.

"Now, why did you need me back here? Why couldn't I stop anywhere?"

Shit. I forgot about that.

"Parker got a call earlier from a... source."

"Parker, the prospect?"

"Yeah." I grab her hand and tug her to the bed. We both sit. I have no clue how to tell her about Jerry, how she'll react to the news that her dad is watching her. I wish one of my brothers could tell her, but she's mine which makes it my responsibility. "Parker's source, Jerry, was hired to keep tabs on you."

"By who?" she demands as she shoots to her feet.

Here goes...

"Your father."

"What?!"

Jaci tries to pace, but I grab the hem of her shirt and hold her in place. She wants me to trust her, so she needs to trust me.

"From what Parker was told, Jerry was hired right around the time you stopped talking to your parents. All he's been doing is reporting your location to your dad."

"All he's been..." She wraps her free arm around herself as if that will somehow protect her. "All he's been doing? All he's been doing?" Her tone raises an octave each time she repeats herself. "Isn't that enough?"

"It is," I agree and wince internally because I'm not finished. "There's more."

I feel like I'm hosting a damn infomercial.

But wait, there's more! For the low, low price of your sanity, dear old dad wants—

"What more is there?" she asks, pulling me out of my head. "You said there's more. You can't say shit like that and then stop talking."

"Your dad asked Jerry to find out everything he can on the Soulless Kings. He knows you're here and that you were here for a week." When she opens her mouth to ask more questions, I tug her to stand between my legs and rest my hands on her hips. "That's all we know, Jaci. Jerry called Parker to tell him about all of it. He's willing to give your dad false information if we want him to."

"I don't want him to tell my dad anything," she argues. "He doesn't get to know anything."

"I agree. And if it were up to me, I'd hunt your dad down and kill him." She glares at me and tries to pull away, but I hold her still. "Don't. I won't apologize for who I am, what I am. If we're going to move forward, we have to do it as the two people we are now, not who we used to be or who we want the other to be."

Jaci sighs. "Fine. But murder? Is that really necessary?"

"Sometimes, yeah, it is."

"I guess we'll just have to agree to disagree."

"If that makes it easier for you, then fine."

Jaci closes her eyes and rubs her temples. "You said if it were up to you... what does that mean?"

"It means that your dad is now involving the club, so whatever happens, however, this is handled, it gets voted on," I explain. "The club made the decision to feed your dad bogus info. That way, we control the situation."

Her eyes open. "And I don't get a say in any of this?"

"No."

Jaci yanks out of my hold and storms toward the door.

"Where are you going?" I ask as I rush to stop her from leaving.

"I'm going to tell your arrogant, overbearing, bossy, egotistical, *unreasonable* president to kiss my ass," she snaps. "This is my life, my family, and my fucking decision."

I block the door by leaning against it. "No, Jaci, you're not."

She cocks a hip and rests a hand on it. "Get out of my way," she snarls, her glare flashing fire.

If looks could kill.

"No."

Tears gather in her eyes, and she angrily swipes them away. "Move."

"I can't, Jaci."

"You mean you won't," she snaps, the salty drops coming faster now. "Tell it like it is, Flash. You won't fucking move."

Jaci turns to put distance between us, but I wrap my fingers around her wrist and spin us around and pin her to the wall. Leaning in close, I lock my gaze on her. As it always does, her scent threatens to catapult me into sensory overload.

"You're right, babe, I won't move," I growl. "You say you want to be here for me, to help me with my addiction, and even to try and move forward with me. You say I can trust you." I brush my lips against her ear and whisper, "Well that means accepting how things work in an MC. Because the club is as much a part of me as you've always been. Don't you dare act like I should choose."

"And if I were to ask you to choose?" she counters, her tone hard.

"I already did!" I shout, my voice like a crack of thunder. My lungs burn as I try to suck in air, and I swear I can feel every single vein in my body throb. "Or are you forgetting how you found me last week?"

Her head falls, and her shoulders deflate. There's a moment where the only sound is our labored breathing, but then Jaci slams her head back against the door and screams. The sound that comes from her is guttural, filled with an anguish that I've never heard the likes of before. It is a scream that will haunt me for the rest of my life and beyond.

Before I can react, Jaci collapses to the floor, sobs wracking her body. I drop to my knees and gather her in my arms, holding her so tightly to try and somehow absorb her pain as my own.

"Shhh," I coo. "I'm sorry, so sorry."

Jaci shakes violently. I murmur reassurances to her, rock her like one would an upset child, and let her get whatever this is out of her system. I have no clue how long we sit there, but she slowly calms. Her hands are gripping my shirt like she needs to hold on to remain grounded.

Flash

"I..." She hiccups. "Please, Wyatt," she begs. "Please don't let them deal with Dad."

I wish I could reassure her about this. I want to promise her that everything will be okay, that the club won't. But I can't. So I give her what I can.

"You won't have to see him or talk to him," I tell her. "This will not come back on you."

"You don't understand," she insists. "Dad will stop at nothing to keep us apart. If he finds out you're a Soulless King, there's no telling what he'll do."

The hair on the back of my neck stands on end, and my stomach fills with dread. Her words hold a level of truth that's undeniable. And her fear is real, so goddamn real that it penetrates and meshes with my own emotions.

"Is there something you haven't told me?" I ask, not sure if I want the answer, but knowing it's the only explanation for her reaction to learning her dad knows where she is.

Jaci stiffens in my arms but says nothing. I maneuver us so I can stand and carry her to the bed. I set her down, and she scoots to the middle of the mattress and curls into a ball. Without thinking, I move to join her and wrap my body around hers.

"Jaci, talk to me," I cajole.

"Allison," she whispers.

My blood runs cold. "What?"

"Her name was Allison."

"Who?" I ask.

But I already know. It's something I never forgot, even though I tried. My eyes dart to the top of my dresser. Fuck, did I try.

Jaci and I used to spend hours talking about what we would name our kids, and she loved the name Allison. So did I. It was the only name we ever agreed on.

"She was beautiful, Wyatt." Jaci turns in my arms to face me. "Allison was so beautiful."

My throat closes, and my own eyes fill. "I thought..." I swallow the bile that rises. "You had an abortion."

Jaci's face contorts, her devastation clear.

"I did. They made me... at five months along."

Chapter Seventeen

Oh, don't you worry about that, Mr. President. I can fucking hack it. Just you wait and see.

Jaci

My head spins as I hold my breath. I never intended for Flash to learn the truth about our daughter. It was a secret I wanted to take to my grave. Not because he doesn't deserve to know, but because the consequences of having that knowledge are irreversible. It's not a little tidbit of information one can just forget. And one of us suffering is enough.

"Jesus."

Air whooshes from me when he finally speaks.

"How..." His Adam's apple bobs. "Why?"

I shrug like it's no big deal, when in fact, it's the biggest of deals. "It took a while to find a *doctor* who agreed to their terms."

"Their terms?"

"Apparently, most doctors don't like being bribed or

performing unnecessary, forced procedures on a sixteen-year-old who wants her baby."

"But they found one." He grits his teeth. "Because everyone has a price."

"They did."

"What's his name?"

"The doctor?" He nods. "Melvin Post."

Flash gets up and grabs my hand to drag me from the bed. I stumble behind him as he leads me out of his room and down the stairs.

"Where are we going?"

He doesn't answer, simply continues to walk with a determination that's almost scary. The main room is full of club members, as well as a few Bangin' Betties. I've met most of them and like them. But the way they're staring now is unnerving.

I try to dig in my feet, but that only causes Flash to throw me over his shoulder. He reaches a table where Fender and Piston are sitting. Without stopping, Flash issues orders.

"Church," he demands.

Fender tries to argue, but Flash ignores him.

"Jaci, what's going on?" Fender asks me when he and Piston catch up to us at the door to the meeting room.

"We're having church," Flash snaps.

"You don't get to make that—"

Flash whirls around, sets me on my feet, and lunges at Fender. He backs him into the wall. I try to stop him, but Piston wraps his arms around me.

"Let them go," he instructs. "It's fine."

"It's not fine," I cry.

"We're having church," Flash barks, his arm across Fender's throat. "Get everyone in here."

Flash

"You seem to forget who you're talking to," Fender growls.

"I know exactly who I'm talking to," Flash counters. "But there's a dead man walking. So you can either call church so we can vote, or there will be an unsanctioned death," he seethes. "Because Melvin Post is out there somewhere, killing babies no doubt, and he has to be stopped."

Fender headbutts Flash, sending him stumbling backward. Flash cups his face, and when he pulls his hands away, they're covered in blood. I struggle to free myself from Piston, but he tightens his hold.

"Let them go," he says again. "If it gets too out of hand, I'll stop it."

Fender grips Flash's cut and throws him into the wall. "You must have a death wish. First, you try to leave the club, and now you're ordering me around. It stops now!"

"Call. Church," Flash demands. Blood coats his teeth and drips from his chin. "Now!"

"P, get the others here pronto," Fender orders. "We'll hear Flash out," he sneers. "And then we'll vote about him. Because this kinda behavior won't be fucking tolerated."

Fender pushes away from Flash and moves to stand at the head of the table. Flash straightens his cut and marches toward me. Piston rushes from the room to do his president's bidding.

"Jaci, you need to leave," Fender says. His tone is calm, but he's anything but. "Women aren't allowed in church."

"She stays," Flash snaps.

Fender throws up his hands. "Any other demands?"

"Jaci stays."

I rest my hand on my man's arm. "It's okay. I'll go."

"No, you won't," Flash snarls. "You stay or I walk."

The two men stare each other down, and part of me

expects to see them produce swords and duel to sort this shit out. Resigned, I sit.

"This is ridiculous," I mutter.

"What's ridiculous is that you've had to carry this burden alone for so long," Flash says. He doesn't look at me though. No, he's hyper-focused on Fender. "What's ridiculous is there's a doctor out there who cut you up and took Allison. What's ridiculous is—"

"Who's Allison?"

Flash, Fender, and I all turn to see Piston walking in with the others behind him.

"Yeah," Joker adds. "Who's Allison?"

"Get in here and sit down," Fender orders. Everyone sits but him. "Flash wanted church, he's getting church." He shifts his focus to Flash. "Now, what the fuck is going on?"

Flash tells them. Occasionally he looks to me to fill in details, but otherwise, I remain quiet, stoic. As Flash speaks, his brothers become more and more agitated.

"Squirrel, get me everything on Melvin Post," Fender demands when Flash is done.

Squirrel opens his laptop and starts pecking away at the keyboard.

"All those in favor of wiping Melvin Post off the face of the Earth, thump twice."

Everyone does, including me.

"Jaci, you don't get a vote," Fender states.

"I might not have a say in how the club handles this, but I get a vote, Fender." I stand and lean on the table. "I didn't get a vote at sixteen, but I get a goddamn vote now."

Surprisingly, Fender nods. "Point taken."

"Got something, Prez," Squirrel says, garnering everyone's attention. "Melvin Post resides in Texas, where he runs..." Squirrel punches the table next to his computer.

Flash

"Son of a bitch. The fucker runs a not-for-profit women's clinic, Prez." He taps a few more keys and then reaches for a remote in the middle of the table. A screen drops from the ceiling and his laptop screen is mirrored for all of us to see. "And that *not-for-profit* clinic can be traced to an offshore account with millions in it. Fucking millions."

"So definitely for profit," Fender barks. "You can make calls on that thing, right?" He nods to indicate Squirrel's computer.

"Yep."

"Get Crow from the Marble Falls chapter on a video call," he demands.

"Who's Crow?" I ask Flash.

"The president of a chapter in Texas."

A few seconds later, a man's face fills the screen.

"Yo, Squirrel, how's it hangin', man?"

Squirrel turns the laptop around so the video includes the entire room.

"Whoa, okay." Crow whistles. "Not a social call."

"We need your help, brother," Fender says.

"Anything. You know that."

"We've got a doctor we need you to bring to us. His name is Melvin Post, and he runs a clinic not too far from Marble Falls."

"What'd he do, if you don't mind me asking?"

"He hurt one of our own."

Their own? I'm one of their own?

Flash squeezes my shoulder, and I grab his hand like a lifeline.

"Consider it done," Crow says. "One question, though."
"Shoot."

"Is this strictly a smash and grab, or are we doling out a little early justice before he reaches you?"

"Smash and grab. He's Flash's kill."

Flash whips his head to look at Fender. "Prez?"

"I don't like your methods, and there will be consequences, but Post is yours, brother. I won't take that from you."

Flash swallows. "Thanks."

"Hate to break up the love fest, but what timeline are you looking at?" Crow asks.

"Is seventy-two hours enough time?"

"It'll have to be, won't it?" Crow chuckles. "I'll get Screamer, Journey, and Poker on it. You got room for them to crash before heading back, or should they book a hotel?"

"We've got room."

"Great. They'll see ya soon."

Crow's face disappears when he disconnects the call. I expect Fender to be angry at seemingly being dismissed, but instead, he looks relieved.

"We've got plans to make, brothers," he says and then looks at me. "Jaci, this is the part where you leave."

"I'm not—"

"Consider yourself lucky to have been in here at all," he snaps. I stand and open my mouth to argue, but he holds a hand up. "I'm sorry for everything you've had to go through. I really am. But this isn't just a you issue anymore. It's a club issue, and I need you to trust us to handle it."

"I barely know you!"

"Maybe so, but that doesn't change anything. You're one of us now, so you better get used to it." He tilts his head. "Or can't you hack it?"

His taunt from the other day rings in my ears. *Because she's not cut out for this life.*

"I thought I proved to you that I can?"

"I thought so too. Don't make me change my mind."

Flash

Oh, don't you worry about that, Mr. President. I can fucking hack it. Just you wait and see.

"Fine. I'll leave. But understand this," I say as I walk toward the door. "Winning this round does not make you a winner. It makes you no better than my father and Melvin fucking Post."

I slam the door behind me and stomp down the hall.

This is my life and my burden. I will not be shoved to the sidelines like some little girl who needs big, strong men to protect her. I've managed this long without any of them, and I can keep managing.

Charlie rushes toward me, but I hold up a hand to stop her and make my way outside. When I reach my car, I connect my cell via Bluetooth and make a call.

Tina answers on the second ring.

"Hey, you," she says cheerfully. "I wasn't expecting to hear from you so soon."

"I need a favor."

Chapter Eighteen

If you fuck this up and utter one syllable that I don't tell you to utter, I'll hunt you down and end your miserable existence.

Flash

"As soon as Melvin is dealt with, your suspension begins."

"And what about Jaci's father?" I ask my prez.

"He'll be..." He smirks. "... *convinced* to leave her alone."

"I want in on that."

Fender shakes his head but faces the rest of the room. "All those in favor of holding off on Flash's suspension until everything pertaining to Jaci and her family is dealt with, thump twice."

I hold my breath and silently pray they all take my side. When they all thump twice, air rushes from my lungs.

"Fine, your suspension will wait," Fender capitulates. "But it'll be two months instead of one."

Flash

"I can handle that."

"Not giving you a choice in the matter, so you better handle it."

"Understood, Prez."

"Is there anything else we need to discuss?" Fender asks the room. "Anything that can't wait until tomorrow," he clarifies.

"I think we need to have Parker make contact with Jerry," Riker says. "The hits just keep coming, and I, for one, would feel better if we get ahead of as much of it as possible."

"I second that," Greaser adds.

Fender nods. "Piston, get Parker in here. Have Royal go cover the gate."

Piston rushes from the room for a second time to do Fender's bidding. He returns five minutes later with Parker on his heels.

"We're ready for you to call Jerry," Fender tells the prospect.

Squirrel stands and leans across the table with his hand stretched out. "Here, Parker. Give me your cell."

Parker hands him the device, and Squirrel connects it to his laptop to make the call so it's louder.

"I was wondering when you were gonna call," Jerry says by way of greeting.

"Yeah, well, I had to go through the proper channels," Parker bites out. "Things are different now, Jer. I'm not the one calling the shots."

"Those biker asshats are wasting your talent then."

Parker chuckles. "Those *asshats* can hear you."

"Do exactly what we tell you to do, *Jer*," Fender snarls. "And I'll forget that comment."

"Who are you?"

"Fender, Soulless Kings president, and your worst fucking nightmare if you piss me off."

"I just screwed myself out of a payday, didn't I?"

"Oh, that depends on how much value you place on your life," Joker says harshly. "I'd say getting to live is payment enough. Oh, I'm Joker, by the way. And I make Fender look like a goddamn pussycat."

"Parker, we're through after this," Jerry says.

"Fine by me," Parker agrees.

Jerry sighs. "What do you want me to do?"

Fender nods at me. "This is your show, Flash."

"You're gonna call Stanley Stine and tell him exactly who the Soulless Kings are. No lies, no stories. Just the unfettered truth."

"Ah, Flash," Greaser says. "I don't think that's wise, and not at all what we discussed."

"Let's hear him out, G," Fender says, but keeps his focus on me. "I'm curious now."

"Jerry," I begin again. "Get a pen and take notes. Because if you fuck this up and utter one syllable that I don't tell you to utter, I'll hunt you down and end your miserable existence."

Twenty minutes later, I finish my instructions.

"Any questions, Jerry?"

"Just one."

"Spit it out," I bark.

"Should I tell Mr. Stine that his daughter is headed south? Or would you prefer to deliver that bit of news?"

Chapter Nineteen

What am I going to do when I find Melvin?

Jaci

"I have an address for you."

I flip my turn signal off and pull to the side of the interstate. When I left the clubhouse, I had no clue where I was going, other than south, to Texas. Now Tina can fill in some gaps for me.

"You owe me thirty-nine hundred dollars, by the way," she tacks on as an afterthought.

"Ti! For what?"

"That's what a bottle of Código 1530 14-Year Extra Añejo Tequila, Double-Barrel Aged, costs... minus the shipping. I'll throw that in for free."

"What the hell?"

"Don has a thing for tequila and has always wanted to try that particular kind."

"What does Don have to do with this?" I ask. Don is a

guy she dated back in college. I thought they'd lost contact, but apparently not.

"You wanted me to get information on Melvin Post," she says. "I suck at that sort of thing. Don, however, does not. He's very good at digging up information."

"I can't believe you're talking to him again," I groan.

"Do you really want to discuss Don, or do you want the address?"

"I'm not gonna forget this, Ti." I sigh. "But give me the address."

She rattles off an address in Burnet, Texas. I know nothing about Texas, other than everything is bigger there, but I assume Burnet isn't far from Marble Falls. That's what Fender said anyway.

"Thanks, Ti."

"You're welcome. Now, are you going to tell me why the hell you needed this info?"

When I asked her for a favor, I was able to dodge her questions, but I knew she'd press me as soon as she could.

"I will, but not yet."

"Jaci, don't make me come after you," she threatens.

"Look, I have to go. I'll probably stop for the night somewhere, and I'll call you then."

Calling her doesn't mean I'll tell her what she wants to know. But this buys me time to figure something out, something that she'll believe and accept.

"You better."

"I will, Ti. Promise."

"Fine. Just... be careful, okay?"

"Always."

"Love you."

"You too."

I disconnect the call and enter the address into my

Flash

GPS. Once the directions populate, I navigate back into traffic, my destination now known.

* * *

My eyes burn as I struggle to stay awake. I'm starving, exhausted, and in desperate need of a shower. I glance at the GPS on my cell and see that the next interchange is only fifteen miles ahead and near a well-known city. I'll stop there.

Forty-five minutes and a quick sprint through Walmart later, I slip the keycard into the hotel door and push it open when the light flashes green. After dumping my purchases onto the bed, I head straight for the shower.

My stomach rumbles as I wash my hair, and by the time I finish and put on the sleep shorts and tank I purchased, I'm lightheaded from hunger. I search for a room service menu and find it near the coffee maker. I order a burger and fries, along with a chocolate milkshake. The person who takes my order comments on the time, clearly unhappy I'm calling so late, but I don't give a damn. I was told room service was available, so unhappy staff can go fuck themselves.

While I wait for my food, I flop onto the bed and flip through the channels on the TV. Settling on a movie I've seen a hundred times, I let myself relax for the first time since storming out of the clubhouse. I know I should check my cell, seeing as I ignored numerous calls and texts from Flash, but I can't bring myself to look. Not yet.

You need to call Tina.

Food first. Then calls and texts.

I don't know how much time passes, but I must doze off because I'm jolted awake by a knock at the door.

"Room service," a man calls out.

After rolling a cart into the room, the man leaves. The burger is huge, and I eat every single bite as if I haven't eaten in days. I devour the fries and milkshake equally fast, feeling stuffed to the gills once the plate and glass are empty.

I push the cart outside into the hall and hang the Do Not Disturb tag on the knob. Wanting nothing more than to crawl under the covers and sleep, I groan at not being able to.

You had the food. Now it's time for calls and texts.

I snag my phone out of my jeans pocket and return to the bed. I might as well be comfortable, right?

Twenty-seven missed calls. *Twenty-seven.* There are four voicemails, but I ignore those and open my texts instead. Flash, Fender, and Charlie have all tried to get a hold of me. I scan the texts from Fender and Charlie before focusing on those from Flash.

Flash: Where did you go?

Flash: Answer me.

Flash: Jaci, why are you heading south?

Flash: You better turn that car around right now.

Or what, you'll tan my hide?

Flash: Jaci, please, stop ignoring me.

Flash

Flash: I'm starting to worry.

Flash: That's it. I'm coming after you.

Flash: Don't do this. You promised you wouldn't leave.

The texts continue, each one more desperate than the last. Guilt engulfs me. I hate that I'm making him worry. But if he gets to make decisions without me, then I can make some without him.
It's not his fault the club has archaic rules.
I decide to end his suffering and text him back.

Me: I'm fine. I'll be back in a few days.

As soon as the text is marked 'read', my cell rings. I don't answer. Instead, I wait until the ringing stops, and then I call Tina.
"Please tell me you're staying in a nice hotel and not some murdery type that you see on Dateline."
I laugh at her. "I am. I even had room service."
"So you ate before calling me," she pouts.
"I did. And it was delicious."
"Whatever."
"Anyway, I promised I'd call, so I'm calling."
"Yeah, about that," she hedges. "Why has Flash been blowing up my phone?"
"You talked to him?"
"As your best friend, I'm insulted. Of course I didn't talk to him. Now convince me that was the right decision."
"He's just worried about me. It's nothing."
"Nope. That's not good enough, Jaci," she says. "You

avoided my questions earlier, and I let it go. But I'm done being nice. Why are you going to Texas? Who the hell is Melvin Post to you? And why the hell does it seem like Flash has reason to worry?"

"It's a mini vacay, he's a doctor, and he doesn't have reason to worry."

"Bullshit," she snaps.

Heaving a sigh, I draw my knees up to my chest. "Melvin Post is the doctor my parents hired, the one who left me without a uterus. He lives in Texas, so I'm going to Texas. As far as Flash being worried... probably because he thinks I'm going to do something I'll regret or can't come back from."

"And does he have reason to worry about that?"

"Maybe," I admit.

"Okay, that's it. I'm coming to you. Send me your location."

"No, Ti. This is something I have to do on my own."

"What does that even mean?!" she screeches.

That's a very good question. What am *I going to do when I find Melvin?*

"I don't know," I say honestly.

"I don't like this, Jaci."

"You don't have to like it."

"I'm calling Flash," she says, desperation in her tone. "Maybe he can talk some sense into you."

I can't stop my unladylike snort. "He hasn't managed to yet. But sure, give that a try."

I hang up, annoyed that my best friend won't just trust me. I don't need people to talk me out of shit. I need them to back me up.

My cell rings, but when I see it's Tina, I ignore it. I pull the blanket over my head, needing to shut out the world for a hot second. When it rings again a few minutes later, I don't bother looking to see who it is before stabbing the answer icon.

"I don't want to talk about it anymore, Ti."

"Where the fuck are you?"

"Flash?"

"Who the hell else would it be?" he roars.

"Clearly, I thought you were Tina," I snap.

"Sorry, babe, it's just me. Ya know, the guy you're supposed to be sticking beside so he doesn't snort shit he shouldn't."

I shove myself up to a sitting position. "Don't you dare throw that in my face. If you choose to drug yourself up, that's on you."

Flash's growl is menacing. "Where. Are. You?"

"Ya know what? I've had about enough of people questioning my every move. If you wanna know where I am so bad, call Jerry! He's the one tracking me after all."

I disconnect the call and shut my cell off. If I wanted to be controlled or questioned, I'd call my fucking parents!

Chapter Twenty

It's a pretty safe bet that if you're within my line of sight, sex is on my mind.

Flash

"You need to take a breath and calm down."

I slam my fist into the dashboard, ignoring Royal's comment. I'll calm down when I'm damn good and ready.

"Dude, you know where she is," Parker says without taking his eyes off the road. "And Jerry will tell us if she's on the move."

"Yep, I will," Jerry adds from the back.

As soon as Jerry told us Jaci was headed south, we mobilized. Parker, Royal, and I went to pick up Jerry and hit the road. Fender is handling contact with the Marble Falls brothers. We have a plan, a solid one.

Then why do I feel like everything is falling apart at the seams?

"We're only a few hours out," Royal says. "We'll be there before she even wakes up."

"Look at it this way, you can fuck her awake. Chicks love that."

I twist to glare at Jerry. "Shut your fucking mouth."

"I suggest you listen to him, Jer. He's a live wire right now, and I'm inclined to let him do whatever he wants if you piss him off enough."

"You're inclined to let me?" I ask Parker. "You're not a cop, you're a prospect. Don't forget that."

"It was just a figure of speech."

"I'm already facing suspension," I remind him. "Do you really wanna push me when I've got next to nothing to lose?"

"Damn, Parker, this is what you traded your badge for?" Jerry taunts.

"Shut him up, Royal," I snap.

"Aw, c'mo..."

The rest of Jerry's words are muffled as Royal shoves a ball gag in his mouth.

"Is that a..." I shake my head. "Ya know what, never mind."

"What?" Royal asks.

"There is so much more to you than any of us know, isn't there?"

Royal winks. "So much more."

"I was right. I didn't want to know."

"Can I help it if I happen to have... *toys* that serve a dual purpose?"

"Yes, Royal, you could," I insist. "Use a rope or a bandana or something else, anything else, like the rest of us."

"What fun would that be?"

I groan, Parker laughs, and the conversation ends.

The next hour goes by in silence. Even when Parker

pulls into a rest area, no one speaks. It isn't until my cell rings that the silence is broken.

"Prez, whaddya know?" I ask.

"Hello to you too."

"Hello, Prez," I mock. "Whaddya know?"

"Crow just called. They've got Melvin and are on their way to meet you."

"Did he put up a fight?"

"The doctor's alive if that's what you're asking."

"Good."

"Send me the address where you'll be, and I'll pass it on."

"Will do."

"Don't do anything stupid, Flash," Fender says.

"What's your definition of stupid?"

"Don't do anything I wouldn't do," he clarifies, exasperated.

"Oh, I won't."

"Dammit, Flash, I mean it."

"Prez, is there anything you won't do for Charlie?"

Fender sighs. "No. No there's not."

"I won't do anything you wouldn't do."

"That's what worries me," he says and hangs up.

I turn to hand Jerry my phone. "Type in the address of the hotel Jaci's at."

Jerry does as instructed. Once I send it to Fender, I slip my phone into my cut and relax into the seat. Now all there is to do is watch the scenery as it passes by.

Three hours later, I'm standing outside room four eighteen, a key card in my hand. Jaci may have picked a high-end hotel, but that doesn't mean staff can't be bought. It only cost me a hundred bucks to get the key.

I smirk at the Do Not Disturb tag. *Yeah, right.*

Flash

"We're gonna grab a few hours of sleep," Royal says as the three of them walk down the hall to their room. "Holler if you need us."

I nod and stick the key in the slot, pushing the door open when the lock disengages. The entire ride here, I rehearsed in my head what I wanted to say to her, but the second my eyes land on her sleeping form, all my anger flees.

I walk toward the bed, and when Jaci mumbles in her sleep, I freeze. She rolls over and tugs the blanket tighter around her body but remains sleeping.

Fuck, she's beautiful.

She was so beautiful, Wyatt. Allison was so beautiful.

I shake my head to clear my thoughts. If I let myself dwell in that dark space for too long, I'll start searching for shit I have no business searching for.

Needing to be close to Jaci, I walk around to the other side of the bed and lift the covers. I remove my cut, fold it and set it on the nightstand before crawling in beside her, and when she shifts into my side, I grin. She may be pissed as hell at me, but she can't stop her subconscious from wanting me.

I turn and press a kiss to the top of her head, and then I try to sleep. I fail miserably though. I'm mentally and emotionally exhausted, but my brain refuses to take a break. Which I should consider a good thing because if I were sleeping, I wouldn't be able to block the tiny fist fast approaching my face as sun streams in through the windows hours later.

"I wouldn't do that if I were you," I say as I wrap my hand around her much smaller one midair.

"What the hell are you doing here?" she screeches. "How'd you get in?"

"Good morning, Flash," I taunt in the highest pitch I can manage. "I'm so happy to see you."

Jaci scrambles from the bed, and my eyes dip to take in the curves of her ass cheeks hanging out of her skimpy shorts. Had I known that and the flimsy tank were all that was covering her body, I'd have copped a feel for sure.

"Oh hell no," she snarls as she whirls around and glares at me. "You break into my hotel room, and you expect—"

"I didn't break in."

"What?"

"You said I broke in, but I didn't." I climb out of the bed and pull the keycard out of my pocket to show her. "I have a key."

"How'd you get that?"

I shrug. "The guy at the front desk was very accommodating."

"I don't even want to know."

"Oh, chill. I paid him off, that's all."

"Of course you did."

She crosses her arms over her chest and huffs out a breath. Her cleavage spills over the lace trim of her tank, and I take notice... along with the rest of me.

"Look, if I'm gonna need to focus on, well, anything, you need to put some clothes on."

"I have clothes on," she snaps, throwing her hands in the air.

"You might as well be butt naked for all the good they're doing." I adjust myself to make my point.

"How can you be thinking about sex right now?"

I smirk. "It's a pretty safe bet that if you're within my line of sight, sex is on my mind."

Her mouth drops open, and instantly I want to fill it. This isn't why I came here, and my anger is still lurking around somewhere, but right now, all I can think about is getting Jaci naked for real and fucking her until we both forget our own damn names.

"What are you doing?" she asks as I stalk around the bed. "Flash, why are... what are—"

I scoop her up and throw her on the bed. She tries to scoot away, but I pounce and pin her to the mattress.

Jaci swallows. "What are you doing?"

"You don't know?" I taunt.

I grip her tank in both hands and rip it apart down the middle. Jaci gasps, and her pupils dilate.

"Flash, I..." She crosses her legs beneath me. "I'm mad at you."

"And I'm mad at you."

I rise up on my knees and reach down to drag my hand up her inner thigh. Goosebumps break out over her flesh, and her nipples harden into pink buds.

"I will stop, Jaci," I tell her. "If you want me to."

Jaci darts her tongue out and glides it across her bottom lip as she nods. "I know. You'd never cross that line, Wyatt. I'm confident in that much."

I bend to touch the tip of my tongue to her stomach. Jaci jerks at the contact but wraps her fingers in my hair and holds me close.

"Say that again," I rumble against her skin.

"What?" she asks breathlessly.

I lick a path up between her breasts, over her chin, and stop just short of her mouth. "My name. Say it again."

"Wyatt."

"Anywhere else, call me Flash," I command. I feather kisses across her cheek and nip at her ear before whispering, "But when we're together, like this, I'm Wyatt. Always Wyatt."

Jaci nods.

"Good. Now, do you want me to stop?" I ask right before sucking her lobe into my mouth and flicking it with my tongue.

"N-no. G-god, no."

"Wyatt, babe." I chuckle. "Just Wyatt."

Chapter Twenty-One

Lethal. This man and his cock are lethal.

Jaci

This man is lethal. Or his tongue is. I can't really tell at this point.

When I woke up and realized I wasn't alone, I panicked. My instincts had me throwing a punch, but that was thwarted. Seeing that the stranger in my bed wasn't a stranger at all incited a fury so intense, I thought I'd explode from it.

Now you're gonna explode for a very different and delicious reason.

Flash pauses in his pursuit and rips his shirt off. My gaze zeroes in on the wall of muscle he calls a chest.

"Like what you see?"

I reach up to smooth my hands over his skin and nod. "It's even better than I remember."

"I hope so," he teases.

Flash moves down my body, his fingertips trailing over

my flesh until they reach the waistband of my shorts. As he continues to move away from me, he takes the thin cotton material with him and tosses them on the floor when he stands. His nostrils flare as he takes in my bare pussy.

"I forgot that about you," he says huskily. "You hate sleeping with panties on."

"I also hate being the only one naked," I gripe.

Flash grins. "Yeah, I remember that too."

He unbuttons his jeans and tugs the zipper down. His movements are agonizingly slow, so much so that I try to sit up and hurry him along. Flash simply pushes me back down and then picks up the pace.

The denim pools at his feet. He grabs my ankles and yanks me to the edge of the mattress before dropping to his knees. For a split-second, I berate myself for not shaving my legs when I took a shower, but as soon as his tongue laps at my clit, all thought flies far, far away.

Flash hums as he eats me, and the vibration is intoxicating. My hips lift of their own accord, pushing my pelvis hard against his face. If he keeps it up, I won't make it another ten seconds.

I grip his hair and tug, trying to urge him up my body. He lets me guide him and swipes his mouth with his arm.

"You taste exactly like I remember." He grins wickedly. "Like everything that's good in the world mixed with delicious sin."

I pull him toward me and seal my lips over his. The first time he tried to kiss me after I came in his mouth, I expected to hate it. I was shocked when my pussy pulsed as I tasted myself on his lips. It's pulsing exactly the same way now.

"Fuck me, Wyatt," I beg as I slide my mouth to his ear. "Fuck me like you used to." I nip at his neck. "Remind me why we're so good together, Wyatt."

He lines up his cock and surges inside of me, filling me so completely.

"Jesus," he hisses. "You're so tight."

"Because it's only ever been you," I admit as my hips buck to meet his every thrust. "Only you, always you."

Flash pushes up to stare at me. "I..."

I cup his cheek. "Don't, Wyatt. Just fuck me. Just... love me."

"Always," he breathes.

The drag of his cock in and out of my body, over and over, should come with a warning. Lethal. This man and his cock are lethal.

Flash shifts and sucks a nipple into his mouth, circling it with his tongue. The combined sensations of his cool, wet mouth and his slick, hot dick, drive me past the point of awareness. I lose myself in it, in him.

When he drags his mouth across my chest and bites the other nipple, my entire body seizes with a blinding orgasm. I experience pleasure I thought I was destined to never feel again.

My pussy spasms around him, sucks him deep. Flash works against the pull, pistons in and out of me until his back arches and he throws his head back on a primal groan and spills himself inside my core. The pulsing of his cock causes a delirium I was unprepared for.

"Ah, fu..." I try to rock my hips, but I have no clue if the signal from my brain is reaching the rest of me. "Holy... Wy... Fucking he... Wyatt."

Flash collapses on top of me when we're both spent, but quickly rolls to the side with me in his arms. Sweat slickens my skin, his dick slips out of me, and cum leaks between my legs, but I don't care. Hell, even if I did, I'm not sure I'd realize it. I'm struck dumb.

"My thoughts exactly," he says in between deep breaths.

"What thoughts?"

He laughs. "Exactly." He raises up onto his elbow and peers down at me, his face sobering. "Has there really never been anyone else?"

I try to pull away from him, but he holds me in place. "Does it matter?"

"No, it really doesn't. Honestly, the thought makes me a little sad."

"Why?"

Flash releases his hold and gently pushes hair behind my ear. Then he cups my cheek and smiles. "Because Jaci. Even through everything, all I ever wanted was for you to be happy. The thought of you denying yourself one of life's pleasures makes me sad. You deserve the world."

Aw.

My heart threatens to burst from my chest. And then a thought occurs to me, shattering it all over again.

"I take it you've had lots of sex."

Why that makes me mad, I don't know. It's been fourteen years since we were together. I certainly have no right to be upset if he moved on, lived his life.

Feelings aren't always rational. And that's okay.

"Depends on your version of lots," he admits. "I won't lie to you and say there's been no one. And I'm not going to sit here and discuss numbers." He kisses the tip of my nose. "What I will tell you is that no woman has ever, or will ever, compare to you. You, Jaci Stine, are in a class far above the rest. And you are the only one who had my heart."

"Had?"

"Had, has, and will always have."

Flash relaxes next to me, and we lay there quietly, both

Flash

lost in our own minds. Minutes pass, and when his eyes close and his breathing evens out, I try to slide off the mattress.

"Where are you going?" he asks as he tightens his hold.

"I was just gonna get cleaned up."

Flash's eyes fly open. "Oh shit."

"What?"

"I didn't use a rubber." As soon as the words are out of his mouth, his face falls. "Oh shit," he repeats, quieter this time.

"It's okay," I assure him as I pull away and move toward the bathroom. "Really, it is."

"No, Jaci, it's not." Flash rushes to me and spins me around to face him. "I wasn't thinking."

"It's—"

"Please don't lie to me and say it's okay," he snaps. "You can't get pregnant and that will never be okay." He shakes his head. "That came out wrong. What I mean is, it's shitty and unfair, and shouldn't be the case. It in no way makes me love you less."

"Okay."

"As for the rubber, preventing pregnancy isn't the only reason to use one," he continues as if I didn't speak. "I'm clean. I get tested regularly. Not because I'm a man whore, but I am an addict. Needles aren't my preferred method of delivery, but I've used them. And when they do the HIV test, I also have them do the STD tests." He shrugs. "It's easier that way. So..." He heaves a sigh. "I'm clean."

"You babble when you're nervous," I tell him.

"Jaci," he growls.

"Sorry. I'm glad you're clean. I am too, obviously."

"So..."

"What?"

He waggles his eyebrows. "Are we good on the whole no condom thing?"

I can't help it. I burst into fits of laughter, so much so that I double over and hold my stomach.

"It's not funny," he pouts.

"It... yeah, it is." I stand up and wrap my arms around his waist. "Yeah, Flash, we're good with no condoms." He lifts me into his arms and carries me to the bathroom. "As long as you aren't using needles," I tack on as an afterthought.

"No needles," he agrees.

He sets me on the vanity and turns the shower on.

"What are you doing?"

"You said you wanted to clean up. I'm helping."

I eye him suspiciously. "Will there be sex involved?"

"Affirmative."

I hop off the vanity and smack his ass before turning my back on him and stepping under the warm spray. I glance over my shoulder and grin.

"Come fuck me, Wyatt. Fuck me, and then clean me."

Chapter Twenty-Two

Try and touch her, see how that works out for ya.

Flash

"We'll be there in ten."

While Jaci was drying her hair with the blow dryer provided by the hotel, I decided to call Crow and see where he and his team were. Knowing they're so close sets off a wave of adrenaline, and I find myself pacing the room.

"And he's alive?" I ask Crow.

Fender told me he was, but it never hurts to double-check.

"He is." Crow chuckles. "Although I'm sure Melvin wishes he weren't."

"Had some fun, did ya?"

"I wish. Nah, I let my boys work out some aggression."

"I can't wait to work out some of my own."

"Are you heading back to Oregon right away, or staying another night?" Crow asks.

"We'll head back. But I made sure our rooms are good through tomorrow," I tell him.

"Figured you all would want a break."

"Thanks for that."

"No problem. See ya soon."

After disconnecting the call, I text Royal to let him know they should get ready to go. As soon as the Marble Falls' brothers arrive, we're out of here.

"Who was that?" Jaci asks when she steps out of the bathroom.

"Crow. They're almost here."

Jaci's lip's part, and her eyes widen ever so slightly. "Oh."

I close the distance between us and wrap my arms around her. "You okay?"

"Yeah." She shakes her head as she speaks, betraying herself. "Yeah, of course."

"Sure about that? Because you don't seem okay."

Jaci shoves away from me. "I'm fine," she snaps.

"You have a funny—"

A knock on the door forces me to pause our conversation. I stride to the door and look through the peephole. When I see that it's Royal, Parker, and Jerry, I open it.

"That was fast," I say.

"Bro, we were just sitting around waiting for you to call." Royal moves around me to enter. "Probably would've still been sleeping if Jerry's phone ever stopped pinging with notifications."

"It's not my fault I'm so popular," Jerry quips.

"You could've at least put the fucking thing on silent mode," Parker gripes. "I was about ready to flush it down the toilet."

"Quit bickering," I order. "It's too fucking early for that shit."

"It's almost ten," Royal counters. "Honestly, I thought you'd be a little more relaxed by now." He shifts his eyes from me to Jaci and back again, bouncing his eyebrows up and down like a horny undergrad. "Ya know, since the two—"

"No," Jaci snaps. "Nope. You're not gonna finish that sentence. Not happening."

"Aw, you're no fun," Royal complains.

"You spent way too much time with Trainwreck," I say. "You're acting just like he used to before Sylvia came along."

Royal puffs out his chest. "I'll take that as a compliment."

"Take it however you want."

"Can we just get downstairs?" Parker interrupts.

"I'm with him," Jaci adds, pointing to the prospect.

After ensuring that nothing is left behind, the five of us take the elevator to the first floor and make our way to the parking lot. Just as we reach the van, which is parked next to Jaci's car, another van marked as belonging to a coroner screeches to a halt behind us.

The driver rolls down the window. "Yo, anyone call for a doctor?"

"Subtle, Journey," I say with a laugh, nodding at the side of the van. "Real subtle."

"Hey, it works." He glances at our van. "It sure as hell beats pretending to be florists."

He's got a point there. I don't know what Fender was thinking when he ordered the custom paint job. The van used to be solid black, but he felt we were getting too many questioning looks. I'm pretty sure Charlie had something to do with that. She always said the thing reminded her of a van that would be in an after-school special about not talking to strangers. Rapey vibe are the words she used to describe it.

It was an apt description.

"I'll let you tell Fender that," I joke.

"No thanks," Crow says as he leans across from the passenger seat. "I'd like to keep my balls. And these yahoos need theirs. Bangin' Betties aren't fans of nutless man meat."

Jaci groans beside me, and we all laugh. Annoyed, she marches to her car and gets in.

"She's still learning," I explain with a grin. "Not used to so much childish testosterone.

"Ah, okay," Journey says. "I can help her with that." He winks.

I move so fast, he has no time to dodge my arm. I wrap it around his neck and yank him forward. I catch Crow's gun pointed at me out of the corner of my eye, but I ignore it.

"She's taken," I seethe. "Try and touch her, see how that works out for ya."

"Got it," Journey mutters. "Off-limits."

"Let him go," Crow orders.

I maintain my hold on Journey until I hear the cock of Crow's revolver. Raising my hands, I take a step back.

"Get Melvin and transfer him to them," Crow orders, looking into the back of their van.

Two minutes later, Melvin is hog-tied and gagged in the back of our vehicle. Poker and Screamer keep their eyes trained on me the entire time they're moving him. Once they're done, Journey parks the van and the four of them move to stand before me.

"Trace?"

Flash

Crow looks over my shoulder at Parker, and his eyes widen. "Damn, man." He grins and skirts around me to hug the prospect. "How long has it been?"

"You two know each other?" I ask, although it's unnecessary.

"Yeah," Parker responds. "Trace and I grew up together."

"You're from Texas?"

"I am," Parker confirms.

"I see you finally got rid of the accent," Crow jokes.

"It slips sometimes," Parker admits. "But yeah."

Crow grins and looks at me. "This fucker hated his Texan accent. Always thought the drawl made him sound like a hick."

"It did!" Parker insists.

"It didn't. You just hated it because it didn't work on chicks for you like it did me." Crow shakes his head. "Shit. If I knew you were prospecting, I'd have reached out. Last I heard, you were still a piggie."

"Nice to see your distaste for law enforcement hasn't changed."

"And I'm guessing, since you're prospecting for a one-percenter club, that your love for that life has diminished," Crow counters.

"Yeah, well…" Parker rocks on the balls of his feet.

"As heartwarming as this reunion is, we've got bigger fish to fry," I say, trying to get back on track.

"Right." Crow nods and then shakes Parker's hand. "It was great to see you. And if you ever get sick of the Oregon coast, hit me up. We'd love to have you in Marble Falls."

"Thanks."

Crow turns to face me fully, and his jovial nature disappears as he levels his gaze on me.

"I understand the need to claim your woman," Crow begins. "But if you ever touch one of my men again, the only thing she'll have left of you is your shriveled up nutsack."

"Thanks for retrieving Post," I say, as I stick out my hand for him to shake. When he does, his grip is hard and unrelenting. "And sorry about that. If you knew our history, trust me, you'd understand."

"Sounds like a story I just might want to hear someday." He drops his arm. "Have a safe trip home."

"We will," I say. "Oh, wait." I dig into my pocket and pull out the room keys. "You might need these."

"Thanks."

Crow leads Poker, Journey, and Screamer inside, leaving us to our business.

"I'm gonna ride with Jaci," I tell the others. "He better be alive when we reach the clubhouse."

"He will be," Royal assures me.

"So, ah," Jerry begins as he rocks on his feet. "When do you want me to call Stanley? I've been ignoring his calls, but I won't be able to forever."

After Jerry told us that Jaci was headed south yesterday, I pushed the pause button on my plan for Stanley so I could focus. Now that we've got Jaci and Melvin, I need to get things back on track.

"We'll do that when we get back to the clubhouse. For now, just text him and tell him you're still working on getting information on the club." I turn to Royal. "Make sure that's all he tells him," I order.

"Got it."

"We'll take the lead," I tell Parker, who will be driving the van. "Stay close. I don't foresee any problems, but ya never know."

Chapter Twenty-Three

All I feel is powerful.

Jaci

The drive back to the clubhouse is long. I drove for the first two hours, but when we stopped at a rest area, Flash took over. Grateful for the reprieve, I drifted off to sleep.

"Jaci, babe." Flash gently shakes me awake. "We're home."

I stretch my arms above my head before rubbing the sleep from my eyes. When I sit up, I glance around to take in our surroundings. I watch as Parker drives the van around to the back of the clubhouse.

"Damn, sorry," I say through a yawn. "Didn't mean to pass out like that."

"It's okay." He smirks. "I wore you out."

I roll my eyes at his smug tone. "Maybe, but don't think that means I've forgotten that I'm mad at you."

"Makes two of us."

We head inside, and Fender greets us.

"Crow called," he says to Flash.

"Let me guess, I've got additional suspension time for what I did to Journey?" Flash asks.

"If I punished every man who forcefully claimed their woman, I'd have no brothers. Hell, I'd have to punish myself. Anyone even looks at Charlie wrong, and I'm climbing out of my skin."

"So, not in trouble?"

"No, not in trouble. Once I talked Crow down, he was fine. Just irritated that you got the drop on Journey. He thought his VP was quicker than that," Fender says and chuckles. "And that's not the only reason he called."

"Wait," I interrupt and stare at Flash. "You claimed me?"

"You bet your ass I did. You're mine."

Warmth spreads through my body. I should be pissed that he's acting like a barbarian, like I'm something to be owned. But all I feel is happy. Because I'm his, and he's mine. It might not make sense to anyone on the outside looking in, but too fucking bad.

"Okay." I swing my finger between Flash and Fender. "Continue."

"What else did Crow want?" Flash asks.

"He wanted to see how Parker is doing as a prospect."

"Did you know that there was a connection there?"

Fender shakes his head. "Didn't even know Parker's from Texas."

"Right? Makes me wonder what else we don't know."

"There's a lot you don't know." We all turn toward Parker's voice and see him striding toward us, a frown firmly in place. "But if you want to know, all ya gotta do is ask."

"Why not tell us where you're from?" Fender asks.

Parker shrugs. "Didn't think it mattered. Besides, I had no clue Crow was Trace. I haven't seen or talked to him since I left for the police academy."

"He said he offered you a spot in the Marble Falls chapter."

"He did."

"Is that something you're interested in?" Flash asks.

Parker's eyes seem to glaze over before he averts them. "No."

There's something there, a piece of information he's holding back. I want to ask him about it, but it's not my place.

"Melvin downstairs?"

"Yeah. Royal's down there with him. What do you want me to do with Jerry?"

"Where is Jerry?" I ask, glancing around the room when I realize I haven't seen him since we got here.

"Bathroom." Parker shakes his head. "Said he had to piss, but he lied. Prick saw one of the Bangin' Betties outside when we pulled in and got a stiffie. I guarantee he's jerking it right about now."

"Ew." I wrinkle my nose. "Gross."

"That's a mental image I could've done without," Fender grumbles. "So, ya gonna get started with Melvin?" he asks Flash.

"I am."

"Me too," I pipe up.

Fender and Flash both turn on me. Fender is shaking his head, and Flash is glaring.

"You are not going down there," Flash says with authority.

"I am." I cross my arms over my chest and tap my foot.

"I suggest you accept that fact because I either go down there with you, or I leave."

"Are you threatening me?"

"Not a threat."

"As much as I want to demand she stay up here," Fender states. "I can't. We've already broken the rules for all the other ol' ladies, why not keep the tradition alive?"

"I'm not an ol' lady," I insist.

"You will be."

"You're gonna be."

Fender and Flash speak in unison.

"Whatever. Let's just go deal with Melvin, and then we can discuss the nature of our relationship."

I walk away from the men and head down the hall toward the steel door that will leads to downstairs. A feeling of trepidation washes over me, but it's mixed with... excitement?

Does this excite me?

Oh, yes. Yes it does.

"You ready?"

I jump at the sound of Flash right behind me and spin around to face him.

"Don't do that!"

"If you can't handle that, you definitely shouldn't be going down there."

"Shut up, and let's go."

Flash enters a code into the keypad, and the door opens. He sweeps his arm forward.

"After you."

With my arms crossed, I march down the steps. Royal is sitting in a chair outside the Nightmare Room, and he's watching the monitor I saw when Charlie brought me down here for Flash.

Flash

"Fender okay with this?" Royal asks, nodding at me.

"I don't know about okay," Flash begins. "But he approved it."

"Are you okay with it?"

"Fuck no," Flash snaps. "But she wants to be here, and apparently I can't deny her a damn thing, so..." He shrugs.

"You do know I'm standing right here, right?" I ask.

Royal chuckles. "We do." He looks at the screen and then back to me. "Have fun."

"Oh, I intend to."

Flash enters another code into the keypad on the wall, and the door slides open. He links his fingers with mine, and we enter the room together.

"I'm heading upstairs if you don't need me," Royal says from behind us.

"We're good," Flash tells him. "Make sure Parker gets Jerry to the meeting room. We'll be up shortly."

"You got it."

I hear their words, am aware of the conversation going on around me, but my stare is locked on the man in the corner of the concrete room. He's battered and bruised, and I can't stop the grin that spreads across my face.

I pull away from Flash and move to stand in front of the doctor. I brace myself for the fear to crash over me at being in this man's presence, but it doesn't come. Instead, all I feel is powerful.

I've seen what can happen in this room. Violent things, horrific things. But I have Flash at my side. Melvin Post can't hurt me here. He's haunted me for years, caused pain that runs so deep it can never be erased. But he can't hurt me. He can't destroy me further.

My lips tip up into a sinister grin.

"Who are you?"

I tilt my head. "You don't remember?"

He dips his gaze to take in my body. "No, I don't."

"Well then, we should get reacquainted," I say.

Flash steps up beside me and wraps an arm around my shoulders. "We haven't had the pleasure of meeting before, but that's about to get rectified real quick."

"Please, *Doctor*," I sneer. "Allow me to refresh your memory."

I take a step closer. Flash does too, remaining at my side.

"I'm Jaci Stine."

I see the moment everything clicks into place for the good doctor. His eyes widen comically, and his face drains of all color.

"And this," I tip my head toward Flash. "Is Wyatt King."

"So nice to meet you," Flash taunts.

"We're the parents of Allison Stine King, the baby you ripped from my belly fourteen years ago. And we're here to set things right."

Chapter Twenty-Four

Mission complete, mama bear.

Flash

"I was hired to do a job."

When I walked into the Nightmare Room, I knew Melvin Post wouldn't be leaving any other way than in a body bag. And I had intentions of making it quick since Jaci insisted on joining me. But his comment, his complete disregard for Jaci and Allison as nothing more than a job ignites my fury to the point of physical pain from how tense I am. There's no way his death will be fast. It will be savage, slow, and incredibly satisfying.

I lunge forward and grab his head to slam it against the wall. "Jaci and Allison," I shout in his face, spittle landing on his cheek. "Their names are Jaci and Allison, and they're not a fucking job! They're people."

Melvin lifts his hands as if to surrender. "Okay. People. They're people."

A small hand rests on my forearm, and I look at Jaci.

She coaxes me away from Melvin, rubs my biceps as I breathe deeply.

"You can't kill him... yet," she says. She doesn't bother being quiet, no doubt wanting him to hear her. "But soon." She lifts onto her tiptoes and kisses my cheek. "I promise."

Jaci rounds on Melvin and shoves him against the wall, her arm braced across his neck. He's not a big man, and he's in his sixties, so he could try to fight her, but he'd lose. She might be even smaller than he is, but she's a mama bear on a mission.

"Thank you," Melvin says, trying to smile through the facial swelling.

"Don't thank me," she says. "I didn't do that for you. I did it for me."

"I d-don't understand," he stammers.

"What the lady is trying to say is that she's going to hurt you more than I ever could," I snarl.

Melvin snorts, and Jaci lifts her knee to slam it into his groin. He tries to double over, but she keeps her arm in place, making it impossible.

"Don't underestimate me, Mr. Post. I'm not that scared, drugged-up girl who you tried to destroy." She tilts her head. "I'll admit, I fell from grace for a long time, but then I rose up out of the ashes of my life and became a woman you should fear."

Jaci looks over her shoulder at me. "What can this room do?" she asks. "I don't see the chains that were here before."

"Ch-chains?"

Melvin struggles to get away from her, and she lets him. He darts across the room and flattens his back against the door.

"They're in the ceiling," I tell her, ignoring him. I walk to the hidden control panel and pop it open. After pressing several buttons, the ceiling opens and chains drop down.

Jaci grins. "That is awesome," she says with appreciation. "What else is up there?"

I tap a few more buttons, enter a code, and point to the ceiling as a cranking sound fills the room. "Well, there's that."

A long bar lowers, and she jumps back so it doesn't hit her. "Damn." She drops her gaze to the floor. "Anything come up?"

"I was hoping you'd ask."

"You're both insane," Melvin cries. He pounds on the door. "Help! Someone help me!" he screams.

"The room is soundproof," I say casually. "But, by all means, continue."

More buttons, another code. A panel in the floor opens, and a pole rises. It reminds me of a stripper pole, but its purpose is pain, not sex appeal. The pointed tip is testament to that.

Jaci cocks her hip and braces her hand on it. "I'm wanting something more, something sharp."

"I've got just the thing." I do what's necessary to open the weapons cache that's in the wall. After grabbing a serrated knife from its pegs, I hand it to her. "Will that work?"

She grabs the knife and runs her thumb over the jagged edge. "Perfect."

I close the control panel while Jaci stalks toward Melvin. He scurries away from her, time and time again. After a minute of letting him think he's winning, she looks at me.

"Will you hold him for me?" she asks. "This is getting ridiculous."

I mock bow. "It would be my pleasure."

Melvin tries to dart away from me, but I'm not playing around. I grab his wrist and drag him to the center of the room, where I lift him up and over the long bar. He scrambles to get down, but I duck below him and wrap the chains around his wrists and ankles so that, even if he does swing himself over the bar, he's still caught.

"Thank you."

Jaci moves to stand at his head and bends down to look him in the eye.

"Comfortable, Dr. Post?" she taunts.

"You can't do this," he insists. "Please. I'll do whatever you want me to do. I'll give you money. Is that what you want? Will money make this—"

He howls in pain when she drags the blade down his cheek.

"I don't want your money," she tells him.

"Then what do—"

Jaci backhands him, and drops of blood from his split cheek go flying.

"I want you to suffer!" she shouts. "I want you to feel the same pain I felt. I want you begging for your life knowing that it won't make a difference." She slices his other cheek. "I want my fucking daughter back!"

Jaci straightens and moves to stand next to the wall. "Go ahead, Flash. Have at him. But don't kill him."

She doesn't have to tell me twice. I lunge at the hanging man and throw punch after punch, unleashing wrath I didn't even know I had in me. Blood flies in every direction as I continue my assault. I make sure not to hit his face, as I want him to feel every ounce of what I'm dishing out. I want him conscious.

When my knuckles crack and bleed and my muscles

burn, I step back to admire my handiwork. He's alive. He's awake. But barely. And I guarantee he's wishing he weren't.

"Watching you like that," Jaci purrs as she steps up behind me and slings her arm around my waist. "It's fucking hot."

Who the hell is this woman? And what did I do to deserve her?

She slips her hand beneath my jeans and boxer briefs. Her slender fingers squeeze my cock, then pump it... once, twice, three times.

"Unless you want fucked against that wall," I growl. "I suggest you stop."

Jaci removes her hand. "You're no fun." She steps around to my front and shrugs. "But you're right. We finish him first and then we can play."

She winks before spinning to get in Melvin's face again. "I think it's time we try something new, don't you?" Without giving him a chance to respond, not that he could if he wanted to, she points to the pole in the floor. "Can you lower that for me, please?"

I do as she asks.

"Would you be so kind as to get him down from his perch? Then you can just drop him on the floor."

Again, I do as she asks and then move to raise the bar back into the ceiling. Jaci circles Melvin's broken body as if contemplating her next move. And Melvin whimpers. His pants are wet with urine and if my senses are correct, he's shit himself.

"I wonder if this is how I looked when you were towering over me," she ponders aloud. "Well, was it?" she shouts as she kicks him.

"I... I dunno," he slurs.

"How much did they pay you?"

"W-who?"

"My parents, you idiot," she snaps.

"D-don't re-mem-remember."

"That's unfortunate." Jaci bends and drags Melvin a few inches to the right. She circles him again, bends down to inspect the floor, then stands with a smirk. "That looks about right."

One second, she's standing there, seemingly proud as can be, and the next she's thrusting the knife into Melvin's gut. She shifts so her legs are on either side of his body and then she grips the handle with both hands and slowly yanks it toward her, slicing open his sternum.

"Flash, be a doll and raise that pole again."

If I didn't already know it, it's perfectly fucking clear to me now that Jaci can cut it as the ol' lady of a Soulless King. She is, hands down, the most loving, loyal, genuine person I've ever known. And her soul is just as dark as any brother's. She's just better at keeping it under wraps.

I press the button to raise the pole, and Jaci moves to stand next to me. As the pole ascends from the floor, the sound of fabric tearing reaches my ears. I grab Jaci's hand, and she lifts her head to look at me.

Tears are in her eyes, the only sign that she's upset. Make no mistake though, her emotion has nothing to do with the man who is now four feet off the ground, impaled on a sharp pole up his ass. No, it's because she finally has justice for her teenage self, and for our daughter.

Mission complete, mama bear. Mission complete.

"For Allison," I whisper, brushing the tears away with my thumb.

"For Allison."

Chapter Twenty-Five

After fourteen years of surviving, of fighting, I've finally gone bonkers.

Jaci

"Here. Drink up."

I stare at the full shot glass Charlie is holding in front of my face, but I barely see it. My mind is cloudy, and all of the adrenaline that got me through the last half hour is gone. I'm cold, exhausted, and utterly spent. This must be what crashing feels like.

"Jaci, c'mon," Charlie urges. She lifts my hand and wraps my fingers around the glass. "Drink it. It'll help."

Absently, I do as she instructs. The amber liquor burns a path to my gut, where it settles like a ball of rubber bands. All of which are straining to break free and wreak havoc on my system.

"You okay?"

I nod.

"Yeah, I don't think so." Charlie guides me to a table

and pushes me down into a chair. "Flash!" she yells. "Get your ass out here!"

When we came upstairs, Flash immediately went into Fender's office. Surprisingly, I was invited, but I ignored them and came into the main room. I'm functioning on autopilot. A meeting of the minds is the last thing I'm capable of right now.

"What's wrong?" Flash demands.

I slowly turn to my right and see him kneeling next to the chair. Black spots dance in my vision, and I blink several times to clear them. That only creates more spots.

Where'd he come from?

"I think she's in shock," Charlie says.

Her voice sort of sounds like one of the characters in Charlie Brown.

Wah, wah, wah.

"Or everything is finally catching up to her, and she's crashing."

Crashing. Yes, I'm crashing. It's all so much, too much. The last fourteen years have caught up, and they're collecting their dues.

Go to jail. Do not pass go. Do not collect two hundred dollars.

A maniacal laugh bubbles up my throat. I can feel Flash and Charlie looking at me, and even though I can't see it because nothing is in focus anymore, I know concern is etched in the lines of their faces. I know it just like I know my middle name is Stine.

Your last name is Stine. Your middle name is Marie.

Then whose middle name is Stine?

Allison. That's the middle name you gave Allison. That way she had a piece of both of her parents in her name.

Allison. Where's Allison? I want Allison.

Flash

I try to stand, but strong arms hold me in place.

Do not pass go. But go to jail. You're going to jail.

Tinkling laughter fills the air. I look around to find the source, but then realize it's coming from me.

I'm making zero sense. There is no sense to be made.

Allison. Flash. Melvin. Allison, Wyatt, Melvin. My parents, Allison, Melvin, Wyatt.

Faces race through my brain, screaming taunts at me. Images and memories flicker like a TV tuned to a station that doesn't quite come through clearly. Every bit of my life is on display like a giant screen at a drive-in theater.

I don't like this movie. I've lived this movie, and I have to say, I'm not a fan.

"Jaci, babe, come back to me."

Wyatt?

"Take her to your room. I'll call Gibson and have him come check on her."

Voices. People. Why won't they leave me alone? I just want to be left alone.

Suddenly, I'm floating, soaring through the air.

When did I learn to fly?

I giggle, and the man holding me groans.

Flying is fun. I should do this more often.

"You're scaring me, Jaci."

Oh, Wyatt. I don't want to scare you. I'm not scary at all.

A picture of a man impaled on a pole slams into my gray matter, imprinting itself and ensuring it's never forgotten.

Huh. Maybe I am scary.

I'm lowered onto a cloud, but then the cloud shifts, and I'm falling. I throw my arms out to brace for impact, but it doesn't come. Instead, the cloud curls around me.

"I've got you, Jaci."

I didn't know clouds could talk. Why does the cloud sound like Wyatt?

"I've got you."

Those words are repeated, over and over. And each time, I feel myself slipping further and further into darkness.

Allison. I want to be with Allison. But Allison is dead. And I'm not ready to die.

"You're not dying."

Wyatt! Wyatt is with me. Maybe we can be a family now.

"Do you hear me, Jaci? You're not dying." I can hear the emotion in his voice, and I try to claw my way out of the darkness, try to reach for him, but he's too far away. "Just rest. I'll be right here when you're ready to come back to me." Something is pressed against my head. I don't know what it is, but I like it. It quiets the voices in the darkness. "I love you, Jaci. You're it for me. Always."

I love you too. You're it for me. Forever.

As the world around me, or within me depending on how you look at it, fades, I realize that I'm not in shock, and this isn't a crash.

Nope. It's much worse.

After fourteen years of surviving, of fighting, I've finally gone bonkers. Every last rubber band has snapped.

Chapter Twenty-Six

A voice from my past fills the air.

Flash

"I'm gonna give her a mild sedative to help her sleep a little easier."

I nod at Gibson, but my focus is on the woman curled up in my bed. When he first walked in, Gibson demanded that I give him space to work. I refused, but with the *assistance* of Royal and Fender, I was shoved into the chair near the wall.

"What's wrong with her?" I ask, my voice scratchy.

"Nothing," Gibson replies. "Nothing physical anyway. This is just the way her mind is protecting her from whatever is haunting her."

"She shouldn't have been down in the Nightmare Room," I snap. "I knew she couldn't—"

"Stop it," Fender barks. "You know there was nothing that was going to stop her. This isn't your fault, Flash. She's probably been fighting this for a long time, and her mind finally said enough is enough."

"I could've prevented this," I insist. "I should've tried to find her. Then maybe she wouldn't even—"

"Don't make me get my ball gag," Royal threatens.

And just like that, some of the tension is eased. My fear isn't gone, not even a tiny bit, but the comment was like a needle lancing a boil. The infection remains, but the relief brought on by the leaking pus makes it a little easier to bear.

"Did you know about his kinks?" I ask Fender.

"Nope. And I don't wanna know." Fender shifts to stand at the edge of the bed, blocking my view of Jaci. "You're a fighter, Jaci. I know your mind needs a break, and that's okay. Take the time you need. And then you come back to Flash. Because he needs you. This club needs you."

He kisses her head, and then walks to the door. "Take a few more minutes and then come down to the meeting room. We've still got business to handle."

"Thanks, Prez."

"I'll leave you to it," Royal says as he follows Fender.

When it's just me and Gibson remaining, I stand and go to Jaci. I sit on the edge of the mattress and lift her hand in mine.

"Will she be okay, Gib?"

Gibson stares at her for a long moment. "Yeah. She'll be fine." He claps me on the shoulder. "But the road ahead of her isn't going to be easy. She's got to deal with things as they happen, or she'll end up here again."

I nod absently. "And what about..." I swallow. "She's an addict, Gib. Just like me. What if she starts using again?"

"Don't let her," he says simply. "You both need to work through so much, but do it together, Flash. Do it together, and you'll be stronger together."

"Thanks, brother."

"Don't mention it." He walks to the door but pauses and looks over his shoulder. "She'll sleep for hours, Flash. It's okay to leave the room."

"I know."

"Okay. I'll see ya downstairs."

Finally, I'm alone with Jaci. I stroke her hair and kiss her temple.

"Sleep, Jaci. Sleep and heal. I'll be here when you wake up."

It takes me another twenty minutes to actually stand up and walk out of the room. As I put distance between me and the shattered woman who owns me, mind, body, and soul, my fear and sadness morph into anger.

Intense, all-consuming anger.

When I reach the meeting room, I throw the door open and barrel inside. Everyone is already here, including Jerry, and all eyes turn to me.

"How is she?" Joker asks.

"Not great."

"She'll be okay," Greaser adds. "She's stronger than she looks."

"I'm aware, thanks," I snap.

"If you need anything, let me know," Riker says. "I already talked to Luna, and we can take shifts to sit with Jaci if you need us to."

"Stop!" I shout. "Stop talking like she's in a coma. She's sleeping. That's it. She'll be fine. We'll be fucking fine!"

I drop into my chair and lean back like I don't have a care in the world.

"And on that note," Fender begins. "Let's get started." He turns to Jerry. "You ready to make that call?"

"I was ready days ago," Jerry says.

His flippant attitude pokes my demons. I launch myself across the table and slam his head into the wood. Gripping his hair, I get close to his face.

"You got a problem with the way we're handling things?" I growl.

Jerry shakes his head.

"Flash, let him go," Fender commands.

I shove Jerry away from me. Rather than return to my chair, I get off the table and stand behind Jerry.

"Call Stanley," I demand.

Jerry lifts his cell, but before he can dial, Squirrel snatches it from his hand. "I'll get him on the line. He'll still see your name in the caller ID," he tells the informant as he connects the cell to his laptop. "But we'll be able to hear better this way."

"Whatever floats your boat," Jerry quips.

I yank his head back by his hair. "Don't test me."

"Flash," Fender warns.

I let go. "When he answers, he's probably going to be pissed that you've put him off this long. Smooth his ruffled feathers, and then tell him all about us. Give him the details of our trip south, tell him about me, and then hit him with the fact that Melvin Post is dead."

"He's dead?" Jerry asks, panic threading his tone. "He was alive when—"

"He's dead," I bite out. "So far, you're not. Don't do anything to end up like Melvin. Trust me, your ass couldn't handle it."

"It's ringing," Squirrel says, garnering our attention.

"Be smart, Jerry," I warn.

The ringing stops, and a voice from my past fills the air. My insides churn, my muscles tense, and my vision diminishes to a tiny pinhead-sized point of red.

Flash

"I pay you too much fucking money to keep me waiting for what I want."

"Yes, Sir," Jerry says, his entire demeanor becoming professional. "I think you'll be pleased with what I've discovered, though."

"That's not Stanley," I say.

"What?" Jerry asks, turning to look at me.

"Of course, I'm Stanley," the man on the other end of the line barks. "Stanley Stine. Jerry, why are you not alone? Who the hell is there with you?"

"I, um..." Jerry stammers and looks to me for guidance.

"You don't recognize my voice?" I ask as I clench and unclench my fists.

"Flash, what's going on?" Fender asks.

"Should I recognize your voice?" the man asks.

I huff out a dark, humorless laugh. "Yeah, *Willie*, you should."

"My name is Stanley," he insists. "Ask anyone. I'm Stanley S—"

"Cut the shit," I boom. "Your name isn't Stanley Stine. It's Willie. Willie fucking King." I inhale deeply. "It's been a long time... Dad."

Chapter Twenty-Seven

What if he needs me?

Jaci

"Hey, you."

I slowly turn my head toward the voice, and my eyes flutter open. Tina is sitting in a chair, which she's positioned as close to the bed as possible. I can't stop the disappointment at seeing her and not Flash.

"Welcome back," she says, and squeezes my hand.

"When did..." My throat hurts when I speak, but I need to know what happened.

"Here." Tina lifts a cup from the nightstand and holds it to my lips. I greedily drink the water, sputtering when it becomes too much. "Sorry."

I shake my head. "It's o..." I swallow, and cough to clear the phlegm. "It's okay. When did you get here?" I search the room for clues as to what's going on but come up empty. "Why are you here?"

Flash

"Flash called me." Tina's expression falls. "Said you needed me. I came right over."

"Where is Flash? Is he done with his meeting with Fender?"

"Oh, honey."

Panic grips my windpipe, holding the air in my lungs hostage. "Wh-where is he?" I push out.

"He left." She averts her gaze, but I don't miss the shine in her eyes.

I move my hand to her shirt and yank her toward me. "Tell me."

"Flash left two days ago. No one has seen or heard from him since."

I scramble from the bed, ignoring the way my head spins. "What?! Two days?" I pace, back and forth, back and forth, trying to call up some memory of what happened. "How has it been two days? I was just with him, Ti," I cry. "He went into Fender's office, and I..."

Nothing. I remember nothing.

Why can't I fucking remember?

"You broke, Jaci." Tina grips me by the shoulders and forces me to stand still. "Whatever happened before he went to meet with Fender snapped something inside you."

Snapped. That means something. Snapped, snapped, snapped...

Oh, fuck.

All the rubber bands snapped.

"Shock," I mumble. "Charlie thought I was in shock."

"Yeah," she confirms. "Gibson says your mind shut down in order to protect you from memories."

I rub my forehead. "Okay. Yeah, okay." I look at her, silently pleading with her to make this better. "But two days? That was two days ago?"

Tina nods. "You would wake up agitated every few hours, so Gibson did his best to keep you sedated."

"And Flash?"

She shrugs. "Everyone is trying to find him. His phone is either off or it died."

"He wouldn't just leave, Tina," I insist. "Something had to have happened. What happened?"

"I don't know. No one will tell me anything. Club business or some shit."

I pull away from her and rush to the door. "I've gotta find him, Ti."

"Jaci, wait!"

With my hand on the doorknob, I look back at her. "What?"

"You might want to put some other clothes on."

I glance down at myself and groan when I see that all I'm wearing are panties and a tank.

"I changed you, don't worry."

"Right. Okay."

I search the room for something to throw on, and then remember that I brought a duffel of my own stuff before shit hit the fan. Spotting the bag in the corner, I drop to the floor and rifle through it. I find a pair of jeans and my favorite hoodie.

After putting them on, I return to the door. "Are you coming?"

"I'll wait here, if that's okay. I get the feeling that you won't get any information if I'm with you." Tina shrugs. "I'm an outsider."

I stomp toward my best friend and grab her hand. "Fuck that. Let's go."

I drag her out of the room and down the stairs. Spotting Fender immediately, I storm toward the bar.

Flash

"What the fuck happened?" I demand before he even realizes I'm there.

Fender spins on the stool. "You're awake?"

"Yes, I'm awake," I snap. "I should've been awake two days ago, but we'll get to that. What the fuck happened, and why are you sitting on your ass instead of out there looking for Flash?" I demand, pointing to the door.

"Jaci, calm down."

I glare at Charlie as she steps up next to her husband. "Don't you dare tell me to calm down," I snarl. "If it were your man out there, would you be calm?"

"No. No, I wouldn't." She reaches for my hand, but I dodge the contact. "But Fender has teams out searching. We haven't stopped looking."

"What if he's dead? What if he wrecked and is lying in a ditch somewhere?" I ask, voicing my fears. "What if he relapsed?" Emotion clogs my throat. "What if he overdosed and is lying in a hospital, unable to tell anyone who he is? What if he needs me?"

Sobs wrack my body, and my knees threaten to buckle. "What if he needs me?" I repeat brokenly.

Tina's arms come around me, supporting me and holding me up. "Jaci, they'll find him."

"You don't know that."

"We will find him," Fender states, his tone harsh. "We will bring him home."

"In what condition?"

Fender averts his eyes for a moment, takes a deep breath, and then refocuses on me. "We will bring him home."

Charlie steps forward and supports me opposite Tina. They both steer me toward a table. The whole thing feels familiar, but it can't be. Because this isn't anything I've experienced before.

After settling me in a chair, Tina and Charlie take the seats on either side of me. Fender sits down across from me.

"What happened, Fender? Why did he leave?"

"I'll fill you in," he says. "But first I want Gibson to check you over, okay? I need to know that you're okay before I pile on more crap."

"No. Just tell—"

"That wasn't a request, Jaci." Fender takes his cell out of his cut and sends off a text message. "Now, go back upstairs and wait for Gibson. He should be there in ten minutes or so. Once he tells me that you can handle a few more emotional hits, we'll talk."

With that, he stands and walks away, leaving me no choice but to do as I'm told.

"I hate him," I mutter.

Charlie laughs. "Maybe right now you do. But know that he's doing this because he loves you. You're family, Jaci. And Fender protects his family. That's all he's trying to do."

Charlie stands and follows in the direction Fender went.

"C'mon," Tina urges. "Let's go wait for Gibson. The sooner you see him, the sooner you can find Flash, okay?"

No. It's not okay. But do I have a choice?

Fifteen minutes later—not ten... I counted—Gibson strides into Flash's room like I'm not about to climb out of my skin with worry.

"Took you long enough," I grumble.

"I see you're feeling better."

"From what I've been told, yeah, you could say that."

"Jaci," Tina warns. "Be nice."

"Yes, Mother."

"It's fine," Gibson says. "She's gotta direct all that energy somewhere. Might as well be in my direction."

His understanding is my undoing. I collapse onto the bed and take a few deep breaths.

"I'm sorry," I tell him. "I'm worried."

"I know. We all are."

"Thank you for keeping my mind intact."

Gibson chuckles. "You're welcome. Other than worry, how are you feeling?"

He wraps a blood pressure cuff around my arm.

"Okay, I guess. I was groggy when I first woke up, but I'm good now."

"Adrenaline will do that," he says. Next, he checks my temp. "Blood pressure is slightly elevated, but that's to be expected." He looks at the thermometer. "Temp is good. You never had a fever, but I like to be thorough."

"Thanks."

"I'm gonna clear you to talk to Fender and help with searching for Flash. Under one condition."

"And what might that be?" I snark.

"Jaci," Tina snaps.

"Sorry."

"Like I said, it's fine. I'll clear you as long as you promise you'll have somebody with you at all times. I don't want you to get caught alone if you start having trouble again."

"I'll be with her," Tina says.

"I promise, Doc."

"And if you start feeling overwhelmed, take a break."

"You said one condition," I remind him.

"Two conditions then."

"Fine. I'll take a break if I need it. But I won't need it."

Tina sits next to me. "She'll be good, Doc. I'll make sure of it."

Gibson shifts his focus to my best friend. "Good luck with that. Something tells me if she wants to do something, nothing will stop her."

"I see you know her well."

"Right here, guys," I mutter.

"We know," Gibson says. "Take it as easy as you can. And remember, never alone, and rest if you need to."

"Got it."

Gibson rests his hand on my knee. There's nothing sexual about it, but I can't help but wish it was the hand of another man.

"We'll find him, Jaci. Believe that."

I nod. "I do."

With that, Gibson leaves. Tina and I sit in silence for a few minutes, but then I start to get twitchy. I need to find Flash. And that won't happen if I'm sitting on the fucking bed, lost in my head.

I hop to my feet.

"Let's go find my man."

Chapter Twenty-Eight

This isn't how things were supposed to go.

Flash

"Don't you have a club to get back to or some shit?"

I snort the line of coke in front of me before turning to Drake. I've been at one of his stash houses for two days now. At first, he hemmed and hawed, not wanting to get tied up with a Soulless King. Something about not being a fan of mixing business with pleasure. But then I found his price.

Everyone has a price.

"Can't go back. Not yet."

I want to go back, to see Jaci. It's taken every ounce of willpower I have not to call and check on her. But I'm scared. Because what if I call and she's not okay? I can't live without her.

And you can't live with her. Not yet. Not until you figure some shit out.

"Line me up again," I demand.

Drake rises from the couch and walks to the safe he has hidden behind a dingy painting of a clown riding a horse. The thing is fucking ugly, but who am I to judge?

"This is the last you're getting from me," Drake says as he tosses a Ziploc baggie of powder onto the scratched coffee table.

I snatch the bag up and dump out just enough for another hit. If he's cutting me off, I'm going to need to use the rest sparingly.

"What am I up to now?" I ask.

"Eight grand. But I'll honor our deal. Find me the jagoff who's skimming off the top of your club's deliveries to me, and we'll call it even."

"And you really believe it isn't me?" I tap my nose. "Even now?"

Drake snorts. "Man, if it was you, you wouldn't fucking be here. You'd be sitting at your clubhouse getting high as a kite there." He shakes his head. "Nah, it's not you."

"You're right. It's not."

"But you have your suspicions as to who it is?"

No, I don't. But that's what I told him. I'd have told him whatever the fuck he wanted to hear if it meant I had a chance at numbing myself.

"I do," I lie.

Drake eyes me suspiciously. "Yeah, we'll see about that."

"Would I lie to you?"

"For a fix? Yeah, dude. You'd lie like a damn rug."

"True," I admit. "But I'm not."

"No skin off my nose. I find out you're lying, I rat you out. Not only to your Prez, but the po-po. I'll find something to tell them that can't be tied to me."

Flash

I scoop a dab out of the baggie, and then I press one nostril closed while I snort through the other.

"You got a serious problem, man," Drake says, judgment in his tone.

"You have no idea," I mutter.

Drake's cell rings, and he leaves the room to take the call. I pull out my own phone and turn it on. I quickly scroll through the missed calls and texts, searching for one name and one name only. When my eyes land on it, my heart skips a beat.

Jaci: Where are you? Please come home. Whatever is going on, we can work through it. Just come home. I love you.

She's okay. Jaci is okay.

I should text her back. My fingers hover above the screen as I try to think of what to say to her, but I keep coming up empty. What is there to say?

What does she already know?

Even in my current state, the voice in my head reminds me of how worried I was about her when she left. I can't do that to her.

Me: I'm ok... home soon... luv u 2

I quickly shut my phone off, ignoring everyone else. Jaci is the only one who matters, and now that she's heard from me, she can reassure my brothers that I'm right as rain.

Yeah, that's not how this is going to go down.

"Shut up," I mutter.

"Talking to yourself?" Drake asks as he strolls back into the room.

"No."

Drake goes to sit, but a knock on the door diverts his attention. He strides to the small window near the door and peaks through the blinds.

"I think this is your guy," he comments. "Kinda looks like that Garth dude from..." He snaps his fingers several times. "What's the name of that show? Supernatural." He nods. "Yeah. That's it. Does your guy look like that?"

"I have no clue." I rise and walk to stand next to him. "Never seen it." I pull the blinds apart to see the person at the door. "But yeah, that's him."

Drake slides the chain on the door and the deadbolt. He steps aside when he pulls the door open.

"C'mon in."

Jerry walks in, his eyes darting from Drake to me and back again. "Uh, thanks."

"Have a seat, Jer," I call, much louder than necessary considering the small size of the room.

"Why am I here, Flash?" he asks as it sits in the chair Drake has been using.

Drake stares at him for a moment. "Sure, there's good." He strolls to the couch and sits on the opposite end from me. "Make this quick."

Jerry pulls out his laptop. "I don't know why you just didn't have me do this two days ago."

"Because, Jer, then everyone would know my plan."

Jerry stares at me, his eyes assessing, accusing. "Your pupils are blown, man. Maybe that's why I'm here and not at the clubhouse. I wonder what Fender would have to say about that."

I lunge at him and wrap my hands around his throat.

"That's a lot of talk for such a little man," I snarl.

"Just callin' it like I see it," Jerry croaks.

Drake pulls me off of the weasel and shoves me back onto the couch. "No killing the turd in my house," he barks. "Do what you gotta do and then you can both get the fuck out."

I glare at Jerry. "I need to know where my dad is. Can you figure that out?"

"I can, but it's gonna cost ya."

Drake whips his gun out of his waistband and points it at Jerry. "It's not gonna cost a fucking cent. Find his dad and get the fuck out."

Jerry holds his hands up in mock surrender. "No need for guns, gentlemen. I'll find Willie for ya."

Two minutes later, Jerry is texting me an address. I turn my phone on to make sure it comes through, and back off once I see it.

"Anything else?" Jerry asks as he packs his laptop back in the bag he brought with him.

"No."

"Yeah."

Drake and I speak at the same time.

"I'm done with him," I tell the dealer.

Drake rises. "I'm not."

He aims his gun again and pulls the trigger. With a fresh hole in his head, Jerry slumps back into the chair, blood trickling down his face.

"Now I am."

"What the fuck was that for?" I demand, shooting to my feet.

Drake shrugs. "I didn't like him."

"So much for no killing in your house." I flop back down and take the baggie out of my pocket. "I'm nowhere near high enough for this."

I pour out a much larger quantity than I'm used to. I

line it up, and just as I lean forward to snort it, the barrel of a gun is pressed against my temple.

"Get out," Drake orders.

"Whoa, dude. Let me hit this, and I'll be outta your hair."

"Get. Out."

I snort the coke as fast as I can and stand, my hands in the air. "I'm goin'."

I stumble toward the door, the high I've been chasing for two days finally setting in. Only took snorting it since the moment I opened my eyes this morning.

"Tell Fender I expect to be reimbursed for the loss of this stash house."

"What the hell are you talking about?"

"Do you really think I can come back here now that neighbors possibly heard a gunshot?" Drake narrows his eyes. "This is what I get for being nice."

"Nice?" I counter. "Nice? You're a fucking piece of shit." I pull my own pistol and point it at his head. "I guess it's lucky for you that I'm here to put you out of your misery." I squeeze the trigger and laugh when Drake falls dead. "Now you don't have to worry about the damn house."

I open the door and stagger down the steps. Walking across the overgrown lawn, I throw my arms over my eyes to block out the sun.

Why is it so fucking bright?

A horn blares, and I jump out of the path of a speeding car just in time. I fall to my ass in the middle of the road, stunned. Flipping myself so I can get up, I start to crawl toward the curb.

Another horn blares, but this time I'm not so lucky. Pain tears through my body as the undercarriage of the car drags

Flash

me several feet and then spits me out, bloody and more broken than I've ever been. It's ironic if you think about it. I've managed to stay alive on my Harley, but a cage is what takes me out.

I'm sorry Jaci. I really was going to come back to you. This isn't how things were supposed to go.

I close my eyes and surrender to my injuries.

Chapter Twenty-Nine

Stupid. So goddamn stupid.

Jaci

"We should probably head back."

I shake my head. Tina and I have been driving around for hours, no closer to finding Flash than we were when we left the clubhouse.

"I can't stop, Ti."

"Jaci, you need to take a break. We both need to eat." She rests her hand on my arm, but I shake it off. "We'll come back out, I promise."

I know she's right, but that doesn't mean I have to like it. "Fine. One hour. And then we keep going."

"Okay," she agrees. "One hour."

I pull into a parking lot to turn around and head back to the clubhouse. The entire time, I grip my phone, silently willing it to ring. I don't even care who calls, as long as someone does. Because if someone calls, that means they found Flash.

Flash

My attempts to call him have been unsuccessful. Ever since he text me back, there's been nothing. He must've turned his cell off again, because all I get is his voicemail.

Tina and I search our surroundings as I drive, both of us tired but unwilling to give up.

One hour. You can do this. Only one hour.

When we reach the clubhouse, Parker is at the gate. He waves me through, not bothering to stop me for a chat like he normally would. I park next to the building, and hope surges as we walk inside. Maybe Flash will be in there. Maybe he'll greet me and explain that this has all been some crazy misunderstanding.

He doesn't greet me. He's not here.

"I'm gonna go plug my phone into the charger," I tell Tina and race up the steps to Flash's room.

I find my charger in my bag, but before I can plug it in, my phone rings. 'Unknown' flashes across the screen, and my stomach plummets. Hospital numbers would come up unknown. The police station number would come up unknown.

"Hello." My voice is tentative, fearful.

"Jaci? Jaci Stine?"

"This is she." I take a deep breath. "Who is this?"

"Thank God," the man on the other end of the line says. "This is Mr. King, Wyatt's father."

"Mr. King?"

"Yes, it's me. I'm sure you weren't expecting to hear from me when you woke up today."

"No, I wasn't. How'd you get my number, Mr. King?"

"I'm at the hospital with Wyatt," he says. "He asked me to call you."

"The hospital? Is he okay?"

"He'll be fine. I guess I'm still listed as his emergency

contact. The last record they had from him was back when he had appendicitis." He chuckles. "Anyway, he was brought in by ambulance after a fender bender."

"Ambulance?"

"As a precaution. He's awake and alert. The doctor want to keep him overnight for observation."

I breathe a sigh of relief. Flash and I haven't talked about his dad, not that there's been time. It's nice to know that Mr. King seems to have pulled his shit together. He was an addict and a drunk. People can change though. I'm proof of that. Flash is proof of that.

"What hospital is he at, Mr. King? I can meet you there."

"He's at OHSU in Portland. But..." Mr. King sighs. "I was going to go grab something to eat. Care to keep an old man company?"

"Sure, I can do that. Where were you thinking?"

He rattles off the name of a diner that's only several blocks from the hospital. I agree to meet him there and end the call.

Stuffing my charger and phone into my pocket, I race downstairs.

"Flash is fine. I'm going to get him now," I call to the room as I rush outside.

I don't even consider stopping to fill them in. I don't want anything slowing me down. Flash is fine and that's all they need to know for now. As I pull away from the building, I see Fender barrel through the door, but I don't stop. Flash is waiting for me.

Well, Mr. King is waiting for you. Get through a quick meal and then you'll see your man.

The gate is open when I reach it, so again, I don't slow down. I careen around the corner, and stomp on the gas.

Flash

I've got miles of back roads before I need to watch my speed in more populated areas. I take advantage of that.

When I'm about fifteen miles away from the clubhouse, my phone rings for the sixth time. I've been ignoring it, because it flew to the floor on the passenger side. Worry niggles in the back of my mind that it could be Mr. King.

What if Wyatt took a turn for the worse?

I pull off to the side of the road and throw the car in park. Reaching for the cell, I ignore the gearshift digging into my side. When I have the phone in my grasp, I push myself upright and answer it.

"Is he okay?"

"Why are you ignoring calls?" Fender barks.

"I'm sorry. My phone fell onto the floor, and I didn't want to stop."

"Who told you Flash was okay?"

"Does it matter?" I counter. "He's fine and—"

"If he's fine, why did I just get a call from the hospital saying he's not?"

"What? But... Mr. King said it was just a fender bender. He said Flash was awake and asking for me."

"Mr. King? Willie King?"

"Yes, he's Fla—"

"I know who he is, Jaci," Fender snaps.

"Why are you yelling? What's going on, Fender? You're scaring me."

"Good. You should be scared." Fender heaves a sigh, and I swear, the weight of the world is in that sigh. "Where are you? I'm sending Royal to pick you up."

"What is going on?"

"Mr. King is who hired Jerry, not your father," he blurts. "Fuck! I should've told you, but I was trying to protect you."

"But..." Tears spring to my eyes. Shit, I'm sick of crying. "So... Flash isn't okay?"

"No, Jaci. The hospital said he was hit by a car. He's in surgery now, but even if he makes it through that, there are no guarantees—"

"Don't say it," I order. "Don't you dare say what you were going to say."

Stupid. So goddamn stupid. Why did I have to get my hopes up? Why did I have to let emotion cloud my better judgment?

"Jaci, where are you? Tell me where you are so Royal can pick you up. He'll take you straight to the hospital."

"I'm on..." I glance around to try and find a street sign, but there is none. Fucking rural roads. "I don't know where I am. Not too far from the clubhouse."

"Okay, Jaci. Just breathe for me. How many turns did you make once you left the property? Do you remember?"

"Uh... four. I think. No, wait. Three. I've turned three times."

"Okay. Good. Royal is on his way. Tina will be with him, okay? And she's going to call you and talk to you until they get there, okay?"

I nod, but then remember he can't see me. "Yeah, okay."

"I'll meet you at the hospital. Lock your doors, Jaci. Can you do that for me?"

"Ye-yes." I hit the lock button on the door panel. "They're locked."

"Good girl. Hey, is Tina beeping in yet?"

I look at the screen and see that she is. "Yeah."

"Answer her call, Jaci. Talk to her until they get there."

"O-okay."

I switch to the other line. "Ti?"

"Hey, honey," Tina cries. "We're on our way, okay?"

Flash

"Uh-huh."

"Why did you leave without me?"

"I... I don't know. I just wanted to get to Flash. I didn't think Mr. King was the bad guy I had to watch out for."

"I know," Tina soothes. "But it's okay."

"Ti, it's not okay. Fender said Flash isn't okay."

"I know."

"What if he doesn't ma—"

Glass shatters, and I scream.

"Jaci! What's going on? Jaci, answer me!"

A gloved fist connects with my cheek, whipping my head to the side, and my phone is knocked to the floor.

"Hello, sweetheart." I turn and see Mr. King yanking my door open. "It's been a while."

Chapter Thirty

I have my life, my friends, my brothers, and my cut. Now all I need is my woman, and life will be complete.

Flash

Beep. Beep. Beep.

Consciousness slowly creeps in, and I become aware of sounds and a flurry of movement around me. I try to open my eyes, but they're heavy. So damn heavy.

"I know it doesn't look like it, but he's lucky."

Lucky? What the fuck is lucky about this?

"How so?"

Fender! Good, Prez is here. He'll figure out what's going on. He'll get them to open my eyes.

"Well, the drugs in his system helped his body not to tense up when the car hit him. He should be dead. Add in the fact that the driver actually stopped, which is rare, and called for help, and luck was definitely on his side. We were able to repair the internal damage before he bled out. The brain swelling has reduced drastically, and I don't foresee long-term effects from that. And the break in his leg was able to be reset."

"Score one for his addiction, I guess."

"That's one way to look at it."

"When will he wake up?" Fender asks.

Now. I'm awake now.

"Likely within a few hours. We did stop the sedatives, but they were being pumped into him for a week, so it isn't going to be immediate."

A fucking week?!

My eyes fly open.

"A..." My throat is dry and my voice barely audible, but Fender hears me and rushes to my side. "A week?" I croak.

"Fuck, brother, you scared the shit out of everyone."

"A week?"

"Yeah, Flash. You've been here a week."

"Where's..." I swallow in an attempt to coat my throat with some saliva. "Jaci?"

Fender's eyes close briefly, and when he opens them, my heart goes crazy. Machines beep erratically, and the doctor starts issuing orders.

"I'm going to need you to calm down, Mr. King. If you don't, I'll have to sedate you again."

I try to take several deep breaths, but I might as well be sucking in sand for all the good it's doing.

"Jaci?"

I flail in the hospital bed, doing anything and everything to get up, but the doctor presses me back into the mattress.

"Mr. King, you need to—"

"Where's Jaci?" I roar, shoving him off of me.

The doctor stumbles back several steps. Fender pushes against me. We struggle for a few seconds, but I'm weak, and can't keep up the fight. I fall back, hating myself for being stuck in this damn bed.

"Prez, please," I beg. "Where is she?"

"We don't know," he finally says.

"What do you mean you don't fucking know?"

"Your dad got to her."

I start pulling on the IV sticking out of my hand. Fender tries to stop me, but he can't. The doctor shouts, and I shout back. There is nothing on this planet that will stop me from getting to my girl. Nothing.

"Discharge me, Doc," I demand as I swing my casted leg over the edge of the bed. My head spins, but I push through the dizziness. "Or don't. I don't fucking care. I'm outta here either way."

"Mr. King, you just woke up after being sedated for a week," the doctor argues. "You can't possibly leave."

"First of all, my name isn't Mr. King. That belongs to a dead man walking," I snarl. "Second of all, I can leave. And I'm going to leave. Prez, get Gibson. He can handle my recovery from here."

"There's no talking you out of this, is there?" Fender asks.

"Would you stay here if it were Charlie missing?"

"You heard him, Doc. Get the discharge papers."

"But he's—"

"Our club doctor will be here within the hour," Fender says, resigned. "He will follow your instructions to the letter. Now, get the damn papers before I cause a fucking scene!"

The doctor scurries out of the room. I have no idea if I'll see those papers or not, but at least Fender has my back. Even if I don't deserve it.

"Fender, I—"

"Don't, Flash. We'll talk about the drug use later. You're alive and it seems that's what saved your ass." He shoves a hand through his hair. "But Jaci is missing, and we haven't been able to track her down. I'm hoping, for her sake and yours, you can help with that. I'm not doing this for you. I'm doing it for her."

"Thank you."

"She's family. It's what we do." He strides toward the door but stops just short of leaving. "Oh, and you owe Lexi," he says, referring to Squirrel's ol' lady. "She got the murder charges dropped."

"Murder charges?"

"For Drake and Jerry. She convinced the detectives that it was self-defense."

Aw, fuck.

Fender storms out of the room, presumably to call Gibson. I look around for my belongings and spot them on a chair in the corner. My cell is sitting on the top of the pile, plugged into a charger.

I hop on my good leg to grab it, wincing when every single movement causes me agony. After powering on the device, I pull up my texts. If my father has Jaci, I think I know where she is.

Spotting the text I want, I open it and feel a sudden burst of relief.

"Fender!" I shout.

He comes racing in, an expectant look on his face. "What? What is it?" he asks, his own cell up to his ear.

"I think I know where Jaci is," I say, holding up my phone. "Before Jerry, uh... Jerry found my dad for me. If she's with him, I have an address."

"Gibson, get here for Flash," he barks into his cell.

"Have everyone come with you. We've got a potential lead on Jaci."

Fender disconnects the call and rounds the bed. Without a word, he helps me get into clothes that one of the brothers or ol' ladies must have brought for me. The baggy sweats fit over the cast on my leg, and the long-sleeved tee is just as baggy so as not to irritate all my scrapes.

Fender lifts my cut off the chair last. "I'm giving this to you, but you should know, it wasn't a unanimous vote to keep you around."

Shame washes over me. "Understood, Prez."

"Not all is forgiven, Flash. Not by a long shot. I meant it when I said we'd discuss things later. Don't mistake me handing you this cut for forgiveness or even understanding."

"Understood."

Fender grudgingly helps me put my cut on. Then we wait.

And wait.

And wait some more.

Finally, the doctor returns with discharge papers. As he's explaining everything to me and Fender, Gibson and the others rush into the room.

"Here," Gibson yanks the papers from the doctor's hand. "Explain this shit to me, Doc. They gotta get going."

"Thanks, brother," I say as I'm being half-carried out of the room by Royal and Trainwreck.

The doctor tries to protest, but it's pointless. You'd think he'd have realized that by now.

"Go get your girl," Gibson calls.

My brothers drop me into a wheelchair that's sitting unoccupied in the hallway. As they're rolling me toward the elevator, ignoring the looks of patients and doctors alike,

Flash

pride wells within me. How did I ever think I could give this up?

I have my life, my friends, my brothers, and my cut. Now all I need is my woman, and life will be complete.

"Is that address far from here?" Greaser asks as we take the elevator to the first floor.

I pull up the text from Jerry and hand the phone to Greaser. "Nope."

"Isn't that..."

"Yep."

"Jesus, this just keeps getting better and better."

"It's the one place no one would've ever thought to look," I say. "It's genius really."

"It's fucking evil is what it is," Riker snaps.

"That too."

Chapter Thirty One

I feel nothing. No love, no rage, no hate. Absolutely nothing. I'm empty.

Jaci

"How are you feeling today?"

I roll over on the cot and blink several times to clear my vision. It's almost impossible with the amount of pain pills forced down my throat over the last week. Not that I can't see at all. It's just fuzzy.

"Not real talkative I see."

"Fuck you," I say, but there's very little oomph behind the words. I don't have enough strength for that.

Mr. King takes a swig from the vodka bottle. He drains the contents and throws the empty bottle into the corner, where it breaks. The first time he did that, I was startled. But that was many, many bottles ago. Not much can startle me anymore.

"That's not very nice, Jaci," Mr. King says as he stoops down to my level. His rancid breath washes over my face, and it's all I can do not to puke all over him. "Especially when I have a surprise for you."

"I don't want anything from you."

"Oh, sweetheart, that's too damn bad."

Mr. King stands and walks to the basement steps. "It won't be long now," he says before going upstairs to the kitchen of the house I grew up in, leaving me alone with my thoughts.

My very twisted, hopped-up-on-pain-meds thoughts.

When Mr. King snatched me off the side of the road, I thought for sure the Soulless Kings would find me quickly. But hope waned with each passing hour, until it blinked out after a full day. I begged and pleaded with him to let me go. I even suggested he call my parents for ransom.

I have no clue if they would've paid because he just laughed in my face. He's been drunk and stoned ever since. Which means I have no more information than I did when he grabbed me.

I don't know why he has me, or what he hopes to gain from this. But I do know that the pills help. At least when he gives me enough, I can sleep. It's a restless sleep, a nightmare-plagued sleep, but it's better than the alternative. At least in sleep, Wyatt is there.

My eyes flutter closed, but Mr. King is stomping around upstairs. It sounds like a giant has invaded the place I used to call home. But no, just a drunk. After several minutes, a familiar sound penetrates the fog in my head.

The garage door?

I remember playing with my dollhouse down here as a child. I would listen for that sound every day so I'd know the minute Daddy got home. Daddy used to love me. Until I disappointed him.

Minutes later, the door to the basement opens and footsteps sound on the stairs. I try to lift my head to see who's there, but I can't make out anything beyond three silhouettes.

"This is absurd."

Mother?

"Why isn't she in her room?"

Daddy?

I shake my head. No, not Daddy. Daddy stopped being 'Daddy' the day he forced me to move away from Wyatt.

"Relax, Stan," Mr. King cajoles. "It's not like I've got her chained to the floor. She has free reign down here."

That's true. I have been able to move around. And there's a bathroom down here, which I'm grateful for. But I've been locked in and force-fed pills. I might as well have iron shackles attaching me to the floor.

"This was not what agreed to, Willie," Father says hotly.

"What..." I swallow several times before I'm able to get the words out. "What do you mean, agreed to?"

Mother rushes toward me. I know it's her by the sound of heels clicking on the floor and the obscene perfume she insists on always wearing.

Nice to see there are some things in life I can always count on.

"Jaci, baby, we're trying to do what's best for you."

She tries to wrap me in a hug, but I summon some strength and shove her away. She falls backward, landing on the once carpeted floor.

"Jaci!" Father shouts. He stalks toward me. "Do not treat your mother with disrespect."

I huff out a laugh. My mind is suddenly clearing. Huh... maybe adrenaline is counteracting the effects of the pills. It counteracts Novocain when I go to the dentist, so this must be the same thing. Thank the heavens for adrenaline.

Flash

Unless it breaks your mind. Don't forget that little side-effect.

"What did you mean?" I demand more forcefully than before. "What the hell did you do?"

"Jaci, baby," Mother begins. "We've been keeping an eye on you. From afar, so as not to upset you," she rushes to add. "Mr. King was simply keeping tabs on your location."

"So you really did hire Jerry?"

"Well, if you want to get technical, I guess so," she capitulates.

"If I want to get technical?"

"Yes, that's what I said."

"So let me see if I have this right." I use the cot to leverage myself to my feet. I sway slightly but manage to stay upright. "You tear me away from the one person who actually gives a damn about me, hire Melvin Post to hack my insides to pieces, then ship me off to boarding school like some forgotten toy." I begin to pace. My movements are slow, but it's better than sitting still. "Then, when I finally get out from your clutches, you hire Mr. King to keep tabs on me. To what end, Mother? What's the goal here?"

"The goal?"

"Yes, the goal!" I scream.

"That's enough, Jaci," Father yells. "Everything we've done, we've done out of love."

"Bullshit," I snap. "You don't love me. And I'm pretty sure you never did. Not really." I whirl on him. "Oh, you loved what I represented. Your perfect little girl, the perfect image to round out your perfect fucking family!"

I turn to face Mr. King. "And you! What the fuck did I ever do to you?"

"You broke my son!"

"No, Mr. King. I didn't break Wyatt." I point at my

parents. "They're the people responsible for that. Their actions broke him. And let's not forget the cocaine you always kept lying around. If not for you, he wouldn't have had easy access." I shake my head, ignoring the nausea it causes. "No, Mr. King. The blame most certainly doesn't lie at my feet."

"Jaci, baby, pl—"

"I'm not your baby!" I yell at my mother. "I'm not anything to you anymore."

"That's not true," Father says. "You will always be our daughter."

"On paper only, Father. Not in any way that matters."

Mr. King turns to walk up the steps.

"Where the fuck are you going?" I demand.

He freezes and slowly turns back around. "I was just going to give you all a chance to sort things out."

"Oh no," I laugh. "You don't get to slink out of here and pretend you're not a part of it."

"What else would you have me do?"

"Make it make sense," I deadpan. "How about that, Mr. King? Make this all make fucking sense."

His face contorts, and I have no time to react before he's on me. He shoves me back against the wall, his hand wrapped around my neck. And surprise, surprise, neither of my parents step in to rescue me.

"I did it for the money," he sneers. "Is that what you want to hear? When Wyatt went off the rails, I had to get money somewhere. This seemed like a pretty easy payday. And it was." He squeezes my neck. "Until you showed up at an MC clubhouse and didn't leave for a goddamn week!"

I claw at his hands, scratch until my nails feel like they're going to rip off my fingertips. My vision diminishes, and just as my body goes lax, he releases me.

I slump to the floor, sucking in lungfuls of oxygen.

"I don't know how, but you and Wyatt found each other," Mr. King rants. "If you just would've stayed away from him..."

"What? If I would've stayed away from him what?"

"That's enough!" Mother yells. "What's done is done. The important thing here is we can take you back to Maryland with us, Jaci. We can be a family again. With Wyatt out of—"

"Un-fucking-believable." I shake my head. There is no arguing with these people. They don't get it, and they never will. How I share DNA with them is beyond me. "If that's what you think is going to happen, you're delusional."

"You will come with us," Father says.

"Or what?"

No one says a word.

"Exactly. Nothing. You will do nothing. Because there's nothing you can do."

"It would be such a shame if we returned to Maryland torn apart by the grief of losing our daughter."

"Is that a threat?" I scoff. "If I don't do what you want, you'll kill me?"

"I'll do what I have to in order to keep our good name."

"And how have you kept it up til this point? Huh? What lies have you told your fancy fucking friends in Maryland?"

"You're unwell," Mother states. "We came to Oregon to speak with your doctors about moving you to a mental health facility closer to us. We've missed you terribly."

"It's been very difficult, but we've prevailed. And now you're coming home." Father shrugs. "Or close to home anyway."

"Wow. Just..." I spread my arms wide. "Ya know what, go ahead. Kill me. I'd rather be dead than without Wyatt."

"Without Wyatt?" Mr. King asks.

"Now you give a damn?"

"Why are you without Wyatt?" he persists.

"Well, for starters, because you fucking kidnapped me," I remind him sarcastically. "And then there's the fact that when you called and said he was in the hospital, you actually weren't wrong. You didn't know it, but he was in the hospital. And I don't even know if he's still alive." I enjoy the sight of his face draining of color. "That's right, Mr. King. Wyatt is likely dead. But it doesn't matter, does it? Because you have money. That's all you truly care about."

"He's not dead," Mr. King says. "He can't be dead."

"You're a day late and a dollar short," I snap before refocusing on my parents. "So, what's it gonna be? Are you gonna kill me?"

Surprisingly, my father pulls a small pistol out of his pocket and aims it at me.

I guess this is what I get for taunting him.

"If it's what I have to do, Jaci, then y—"

I scream as my father slumps to the floor, blood oozing from a hole in his head.

"Jaci is not dying today," Fender snarls as he steps over my dead father. "Not on my goddamn watch."

My mother tries to run around Fender, but he snags her around the waist and presses his gun to her temple.

"It's your call, Jaci," he says casually.

"Where's Flash?" I blurt, asking the only thing I give a damn about.

"He's upstairs. Didn't want to waste time dragging a wheelchair down here."

Mr. King gasps at this new information and makes a mad dash for the stairs. Joker meets him, with his gun trained on the drunk.

Flash

"Not so fast." Joker grins. "Turns out, your son doesn't really give a damn what happens to you. So please, *please*, give me a reason to pull this trigger."

"No. No. I won't cause any—"

"He's been drugging me for the last week," I tell them.

"Thank you, Jaci. You just made my day."

Joker squeezes the trigger, and Mr. King falls to the floor with a hole identical to my father's.

"Jaci, baby, please," Mother begs. "Don't do this. I love—"

"Just say the word, Jaci," Fender says.

I stare at my mother, the woman who gave me life. And I feel nothing. No love, no rage, no hate. Absolutely nothing. I'm empty where she's concerned.

It would be so easy to let her die. But what would that accomplish? More bloodshed, sure. More death and mayhem.

Would you feel better if she dies?

I'd love to say yes. It would be easy to say yes. I want to say yes.

But death is too easy for a woman like Janice Stine. Being alone, ripped from the rich world she fancies herself a part of? That would be hell on Earth.

"Can you have her locked away in a mental institution?" I ask, the idea gaining momentum in my mind the longer I think about it. "No visitors, no calls, no contact with anyone, ever? Can you do that, Fender? Can you make that happen?"

"I can."

"Then she can live."

"Joker, take her," Fender commands as he shoves my mother at his brother in leather.

With the danger eliminated, my adrenaline fades. My head spins, and the world darkens.

"Fender?"

"Yeah."

"I'm gonna pass out now," I mumble.

I have no idea if I hit the floor or not because the next thing I know, I'm opening my eyes and staring at the best sight of my life.

"Hey, babe."

"Flash?" I reach up and touch his cheek. "You're really here."

"I'm really here," he confirms.

"And I'm not dead? We're not dead? Because that would be just our luck, ya know."

Flash laughs, and the sound lights me up from the inside out.

"No, Jaci, we are definitely not dead."

"Good." I close my eyes. "Can we go home now?"

"No."

My eyes fly open at Fender's voice.

"Why not?" Flash asks. "We're done here, right?"

"We are. But neither of you are going home."

"Please, Fender," I plead. "I'm tired."

"I know you are. I'm sure you both are. But you're going to rehab." He focuses on Flash. "I told you we'd deal with your addiction once we got your girl. Well, we got your girl. You're going back to YGT. The new therapist is anxious to get started with you."

"Okay, Prez."

Fender narrows his eyes. "No argument?"

"No," Flash confirms. "I need to go. I don't ever want to let Jaci down again, and if we really want a future together, rehab is the first step."

"Good."

"What about me?" I ask.

"You're going to another facility that Tina found. I know you didn't willingly take the pills, but we all want you as well as you can be. This whole experience has been traumatic, and with the whole—"

"I'll go, Fender," I tell him. 'You don't have to justify anything to me. If Flash is going, so am I. I'll miss him. Hell, I'll miss all of you. But I'll be better for it. And so will he."

"See, Prez, we're not too hard to handle," Flash jokes.

"Uh-huh," Fender says. "You've got thirty minutes before you're both picked up to go your separate ways. Make the most of your time. And for fuck's sake, no screwing. Neither of you are in any condition for that."

Fender walks away, leaving me alone in Flash's lap.

"I'm so sorry, Jaci. I lost myself there for a while. But I—"

"Do you love me?"

"Yes."

"I love you too." I press a soft kiss to his lips.

"You're it for me, Jaci. Always."

"And you're it for me, Wyatt. Forever."

Epilogue

We really are angels.

Flash

Six months later...

"Are you sure you can't see anything?"

Jaci bounces on her feet beside me. I can't see her, but I can feel her boobs along my arm.

"I'm sure." I reach toward her, grabbing a handful of tit. "But I feel something."

"Flash," she cries and shoves my hand away. "We're in public."

"Well how am I supposed to know that? You've had me blindfolded since we left the clubhouse."

We've been staying in my room there while our house is being built. Jaci and I both completed our respective rehab programs. She was in for twenty-one days, while I was at YGT for sixty. When she picked me up, we went straight to the courthouse and got married.

The program says relationships aren't good for addicts

in recovery. And I get that. I really do. But our addictions stemmed from us being apart. There was never going to be anyone else for either of us, so getting married was the only option.

As soon as we showed him the marriage certificate, Fender gave us a wedding gift: my suspension. Two more months away from the club. But it wasn't all bad. Jaci and I were able to take a honeymoon to the Caribbean, and then she focused on getting back to work.

"Just stop being such a horn dog," she quips. "We're almost there."

I walk slowly as my wife leads me around, warning me about dips and obstacles every few feet. She once asked me if I trusted her. I told her then that I did. And if allowing her to blindly lead me around in a public place doesn't prove that, I don't know what will.

"Okay." Jaci spins me around and then grabs my hand. "We're here."

"So I can take this thing off?"

Her sigh is loud, and her hand is shaking.

"Jaci? What's wrong?"

"I'm so nervous," she admits. "I've never shared this with anyone." Her shoulder brushes my arm when she shrugs. "But this place... it's not for me. Not just me anyway. It's for us."

"Jaci, babe, please take this stupid thing off me." I squeeze her hand. "I don't like it when I can't see your face, especially when I can hear the pain in your voice."

She moves to stand behind me. Her small hands work the knot at the back of my head until the blindfold falls away.

Emotion clogs my throat as my eyes land on the headstone before me. Jace returns to my side.

"Wyatt, meet Allison," she says. "Allison, my love, meet your daddy."

Tears silently stream down my cheeks. "How? When? My baby girl."

Jaci wraps her arms around my waist, and I hug her to my side.

"As soon as I had the money saved up, I had the headstone made," she explains. "I used to come here a lot, especially when life got me down."

"Allison Stine King," I read aloud. Then I notice the date. "Wait. Is today..."

"Fifteen years ago today, yes," she confirms. "You should know, she's not really here. I don't know what happened after... well, after. But her spirit is here, I think. I feel her here."

I tip my head back and look to the sky. Clouds shift across the blue expanse. The breeze kicks up, and my beard sways the tiniest bit.

"She's here," I say. "I feel her."

Jaci and I sit in the grass. I pull her between my legs and hold her tight. I don't know how she ever faced this alone, but I'm so grateful that she did. Because without her, I wouldn't have this connection to Allison.

"I don't wanna go."

Jaci and I both turn toward the pouted words. Standing about forty feet away, at another headstone, is a little girl. She's currently trying to pull away from the woman holding her hand, but she's not getting anywhere.

"Honey, we have to," the woman says. "But I'll bring you back soon."

"No," the girl cries as she stomps her foot. "I want my mommy."

"Oh God," Jaci whispers.

Flash

The little girl kicks the woman in the shin and darts toward us.

"Ali," the woman yells. "Get back here."

I watch as the woman chases after her. When Ali is close enough, I lean back and lift her above my head.

"Hey munchkin," I say with a smile.

"I am so sorry," the woman says and lifts Ali from my hands. "She's having a hard time lately."

"No problem." I nod toward the headstone they were in front of. "Mom?"

"Sadly, yes."

"Why is my name on the stone?" Ali asks, pointing to Allison's headstone.

Jaci gasps.

"Well, sweetie, Allison was our daughter," Jaci explains patiently. "And only very special little girls have a name as beautiful as Allison. You must be very special."

"My mommy always said I was special." Ali rubs her eyes. "Mommy's not coming back."

"I'm so sorry to hear that, sweetie. I bet she loved you very much."

Ali nods.

"Again, I'm sorry to have disturbed you," the woman says. "Ali, we really need to go."

Ali digs in her heels. "I'm five," she says proudly, holding up four fingers.

I reach out and lift her pinky finger. "There ya go, munchkin. Now you're five."

"Oh, right. Mommy was still teaching me numbers." She screws her face up, and it's the most adorable thing I've ever seen. "She said I'm smart."

"You are smart," Jaci exclaims. "I can see that."

"You can?"

"I sure can, sweetie."

"Do you need a little girl?" Ali asks, all the innocence of a child in her tone. "Mommy said that angels would find me because angels needs little girls. Are you angels that need a little girl?"

Jaci and I exchange a look. This is the most unconventional conversation I've ever had in my life, and it's filling my heart with so much joy.

Jaci's made me soft. And I love it.

"Ali," the woman admonishes. "We'll find you some angels, okay? Let's let these nice people get—"

"Wait," Jaci says. "Um..." She looks at me again, questions dancing in her eyes. I nod. "Do you have a business card?"

"I, um..." She reaches into her pocket and then hands a card to Jaci. "I'm Bonnie, by the way. And you've met Ali." She shakes her head. "I'm sorry, this just isn't at all what I was expecting when I picked her up from her foster home today."

"Well, we do very well with the unexpected, don't we?" I say, smiling at Jaci.

"I don't know how this works, or..." Jaci laughs. "Can we maybe come talk to you on Monday? Would that be okay?"

"You are angels," Ali exclaims. "Mommy was right."

"I..." I wince at her excitement. I don't want to get her hopes up. Especially not when this is a completely chance meeting at a cemetery. "Ali, we might be angels. But even angels have to, um..."

"Angels have a screening process," Bonnie says quickly, saving me. "Because little girls need to have the very best angels looking after them. So, let's see if they pass their angel tests, okay?"

Flash

Ali jumps up and down, clapping her hands. "Yay. I might get my angels." She races back to her mother's grave and shouts, "Did you hear that Mommy? I might get angels. And they said only very special girls are named Allison."

"I'm sorry, but are you serious?" Bonnie asks in a hushed tone so Ali doesn't overhear. "I've never had this happen before. And Ali, she's been through a lot. Too much, really. And I don't want her to get her hopes up if—"

"Bonnie," Jaci interrupts.

"Yes?"

"Breathe. You clearly care about Ali, even if you're only her social worker. And I admire that." Jaci grabs Bonnie's hand. "Yes, we're serious. Angels come in all types of packages and when you least expect them."

"Right. You're right." Bonnie nods, smiling brightly for the first time. "I get to the office around eight on Mondays. I hope to see you then."

She walks to Ali, and Jaci and I watch as they head toward the parking lot.

"Did that just happen?" I ask.

"I think so." Jaci grabs my hand and places it on her arm. "Pinch me, please. I need to know I'm not dreaming."

I don't pinch her. Instead I lift her in my arms and spin her around, kissing her lips mercilessly until we're both breathless.

"Angels," I say when I set her back on her feet. "I like it."

And it turns out, we really are angels. Ali's angels who needed a very special little girl to love.

Next in the Soulless Kings MC Series

Royal: Book 10

Royal...

My patch is everything to me. It signifies all that I've sacrificed for, all that I did as a prospect, everything I've ever wanted. Not only was I voted into the Soulless Kings MC as a patched member, but I'm now in charge of recruiting new prospects. And I'm damn good at it... until one night, one bad decision threatens my world.

Next in the Soulless Kings MC Series

Fortunately, I have someone looking out for me. No, it's not who you'd expect, but it's someone far better than I could have hoped for. Paige isn't the chick who caught my eye, but she is the one who saves me from myself. As much as I don't want to believe what she tells me, I don't seem to have a choice. Because every time I turn around, the object of her warning is always there, waiting, watching, planning. And I vow to do whatever it takes to keep Paige, and my club, safe from their destruction.

Paige...

I'm not exactly what you'd call a hot commodity. I'm not the woman who catches a man's eye or even one who drunks hook up with for one night of fun. No, all of that's reserved for my best friend. The problem with that is she's not single. She doesn't care who she hurts in the process, as long as she gets what she wants.

But I'm done protecting her, lying for her. Her latest mark is someone who could easily cause a lot of damage to all involved, but there's something about his eyes that draws me in, makes me see him for more than what he flashes on the outside. He's not a bad guy, just a horny one. He may have had his sights set on my friend, but once I tell him the truth, I'm the woman he sinks his fingers into, literally and figuratively. I can only hope he doesn't eventually deem me guilty by association.

About the Author

Andi Rhodes is an author whose passion is creating romance from chaos in all her books! She writes MC (motorcycle club) romance with a generous helping of suspense and doesn't shy away from the more difficult topics. Her books can be triggering for some so consider yourself warned. Andi also ensures each book ends with the couple getting their HEA! Most importantly, Andi is living her real life HEA with her husband and their boxers.

For access to release info, updates, and exclusive content, be sure to sign up for Andi's newsletter at andirhodes.com.

Also by Andi Rhodes

Broken Rebel Brotherhood

Broken Souls

Broken Innocence

Broken Boundaries

Broken Rebel Brotherhood: Complete Series Box set

Broken Rebel Brotherhood: Next Generation

Broken Hearts

Broken Wings

Broken Mind

Bastards and Badges

Stark Revenge

Slade's Fall

Jett's Guard

Soulless Kings MC

Fender

Joker

Piston

Greaser

Riker

Trainwreck

Squirrel

Gibson

Flash

Royal

Satan's Legacy MC

Snow's Angel

Toga's Demons

Magic's Torment

Duck's Salvation

Dip's Flame

Devil's Handmaidens MC

Harlow's Gamble

Peppermint's Twist

Mama's Rules

Valhalla Rising MC

Viking

Mayhem Makers

Forever Savage

Saints Purgatory MC

Unholy Soul

Printed in Great Britain
by Amazon

44178522R00131